BATTER UP

Fargo walked on to Chatterly's. He opened the gate and went to the steps and up them to the front door. He didn't bother to knock but walked on in and made for the kitchen.

He was almost to the parlor when Harvey Stansfield stepped out in front of him. Harvey was holding a new ax handle. In the parlor stood McNee and Dugan with ax handles of their own.

"Hell," Fargo said.

"We have you now, you son of a bitch," Harvey declared.

"Were you born stupid or do you work at it?"

Harvey roared like a shot bear and raised the handle like a club. A near-maniacal expression came over him and he swung at Fargo's head. : . .

THE
TRAILSMAN
#350

HIGH
COUNTRY
HORROR

by

Jon Sharpe

A SIGNET BOOK

SIGNET
Published by New American Library, a division of
Penguin Group (USA) Inc., 375 Hudson Street,
New York, New York 10014, USA
Penguin Group (Canada), 90 Eglinton Avenue East, Suite 700, Toronto,
Ontario M4P 2Y3, Canada (a division of Pearson Penguin Canada Inc.)
Penguin Books Ltd., 80 Strand, London WC2R 0RL, England
Penguin Ireland, 25 St. Stephen's Green, Dublin 2,
Ireland (a division of Penguin Books Ltd.)
Penguin Group (Australia), 250 Camberwell Road, Camberwell, Victoria 3124,
Australia (a division of Pearson Australia Group Pty. Ltd.)
Penguin Books India Pvt. Ltd., 11 Community Centre, Panchsheel Park,
New Delhi - 110 017, India
Penguin Group (NZ), 67 Apollo Drive, Rosedale, North Shore 0632,
New Zealand (a division of Pearson New Zealand Ltd.)
Penguin Books (South Africa) (Pty.) Ltd., 24 Sturdee Avenue,
Rosebank, Johannesburg 2196, South Africa

Penguin Books Ltd., Registered Offices:
80 Strand, London WC2R 0RL, England

First published by Signet, an imprint of New American Library,
a division of Penguin Group (USA) Inc.

First Printing, December 2010
10 9 8 7 6 5 4 3 2 1

The first chapter of this book previously appeared in *New Mexico Gun-Down*, the three
hundred forty-ninth volume in this series.

Copyright © Penguin Group (USA) Inc., 2010
All rights reserved

Ⓟ REGISTERED TRADEMARK—MARCA REGISTRADA

Printed in the United States of America

The Trailsman

Beginnings . . . they bend the tree and they mark the man. Skye Fargo was born when he was eighteen. Terror was his midwife, vengeance his first cry. Killing spawned Skye Fargo, ruthless, cold-blooded murder. Out of the acrid smoke of gunpowder still hanging in the air, he rose, cried out a promise never forgotten.

The Trailsman they began to call him all across the West: searcher, scout, hunter, the man who could see where others only looked, his skills for hire but not his soul, the man who lived each day to the fullest, yet trailed each tomorrow. Skye Fargo, the Trailsman, the seeker who could take the wildness of a land and the wanting of a woman and make them his own.

*Arizona Territory, 1863—where death comes
in the dark of night, and worse in the bright light of day.*

Skye Fargo was snapped out of a sound sleep by a whinny from the Ovaro.

He rose onto his elbows and gazed about his camp. The fire had nearly gone out; only a few embers glowed red. Overhead, a legion of stars sparkled like gems.

Inky shadows shrouded the surrounding woods. He glanced at the Ovaro.

"What did you do that for?"

The stallion seldom whinnied without cause. Fargo went on looking and listening and when nothing happened he rolled onto his side and pulled his blanket up.

They were high on the Mogollon Plateau in wild country, and it was early autumn. At that time of year the night air was chill.

No sooner did Fargo close his eyes than a far-off drumming caused him to open them again. He sat up, put his hat on, and rose. A big man, broad of shoulder and narrow of waist, he wore buckskins and boots and had a red bandanna around his neck. Bending, Fargo plucked his gun belt from the ground and strapped it on.

The drumming grew louder. Fargo stepped away from the embers to the edge of the trees so he was in darkness and put his hand on his Colt. It paid to be cautious where night riders were concerned. He reckoned there must have been half a dozen or more and he was proven right when eight riders came along the rutted dirt track that was called a road in these parts, and drew rein at the clearing's edge.

"Lookee here," a man declared.

"A horse," another said.

They reined into the clearing. One man dismounted and stepped to where Fargo's saddle and blankets lay. "Someone was sleeping here but they're gone."

"No," Fargo said. "They're not." He showed himself, demanding, "Who are you and what do you want?"

The man who had dismounted swooped his hand to his revolver but before he could clear leather Fargo slicked the Colt and trained it on him. They all heard the click of the hammer.

"Try to jerk that six-shooter and you're dead," Fargo warned.

"Hold on, Harvey," said one of those on horseback. "Let's not provoke him. We could be mistaken."

"Take your hand off that six-shooter," Fargo said.

The man called Harvey scowled but complied.

Fargo kept his Colt on the would-be quick draw artist and came closer. He had thought maybe they were cowboys but several wore suits and bowlers or derbies and others wore store-bought shirts and britches or homespun.

Townsmen and farmers, he reckoned. "What the hell is this about?"

"As if you don't know," said Harvey.

"I wouldn't rile me more than you have," Fargo told him.

Harvey was almost as tall as Fargo and a lot thicker through the middle. He wore a bowler atop curly hair that framed a square block of a face with a nose as big as a cucumber. His suit included a vest from which a gold watch chain dangled. "I don't like some saddle tramp telling me what to do."

"Harvey, please," said the rider who had spoken before. "Let me handle this, will you?"

"Sure, Tom," Harvey said. "Kiss his ass, why don't you?"

The rider kneed his horse a little closer. "I'm sorry, mis-

2

ter, to barge in on you like this, but it's a matter of life and death. My name is Tom Wilson. We're all of us from Haven."

Fargo recollected a town by that name. Several had sprung up in the past few years in the deep valleys that penetrated the Mogollon Plateau. "What are you doing here?"

"We're hunting for a missing girl," Wilson said. "A young woman, actually. She's nineteen years old. Her name is Myrtle Spencer and she was wearing a blue dress when she was seen last."

"What do you mean, missing?"

The man called Harvey growled, "As if you don't know, you son of a bitch. Where is she?"

"Harvey," Wilson said. "You're not helping matters."

"I don't care." Harvey gestured angrily at Fargo. "I say we make him tell us what he did with her. And if he won't tell, then we string him up."

"I don't know any Myrtle Spencer," Fargo said.

Two other riders were edging their hands toward holsters. They were trying to be sneaky about it but they were as obvious as a charging buffalo.

Fargo took another step and extended the Colt so the muzzle gouged Harvey's brow. "I won't say this again. Tell your friends to sit real still while we sort this out or I will by-God splatter your brains."

Harvey stiffened. He glared at Fargo, then said, "You heard him, boys. Don't try anything. We'll hear what the bastard has to say."

Wilson turned to the other two. "Dugan. McNee. You're not helping matters. Let me do the talking and you behave yourselves." He smiled at Fargo. "My apologies, mister. But we're high-strung over that missing girl. She's as sweet as can be and we would hate for anything to happen to her."

"I don't know any Myrtle Spencer," Fargo repeated himself.

"That may be. But you wouldn't have to know her to abduct her," Wilson said.

"Do you see a woman around here anywhere?" Fargo asked in mild exasperation. "Use your damn heads."

"That's what I'm trying to do," Wilson said. "Would you mind terribly much if me and a few of the rest were to look around?"

"Suit yourselves," Fargo said. "But keep your hands away from your hardware." He nodded at Dugan and McNee. "All of you can look except those two and this one." He tapped the Colt against Harvey's forehead. "I want them where I can keep an eye on them."

"Hell," Harvey said.

"You brought it on yourself, Harve," Wilson said. He climbed down and commenced walking about the clearing. Two others, at his urging, went into the trees. They were back in a couple of minutes, shaking their heads. One of them said, "Not a sign of her."

Wilson turned to Fargo. "Would you care to explain who you are and what you're doing here?"

"That's none of your business." Fargo didn't poke his nose into the affairs of others and he would be damned if he would let anyone poke their nose into his.

"Please," Wilson said. "It's important. If you've done nothing wrong you have no reason to worry."

Fargo was trying to be reasonable. He resented Harvey but there *was* a woman missing, or so they claimed. "Don't you have a lawman in Haven?"

"Yes, we do, in fact. Marshal Tibbit. He is out with another search party. They went north and we came south." Wilson turned to the others. "I have an idea. Why don't one of you fetch the marshal while we keep an eye on this gentleman? Lawrence, would you mind?"

"No," a townsman said. "I'll be back as quick as I can." Reining around, he jabbed his heels against his animal and trotted up the road.

"Now then," Wilson said. "Why don't the rest of us make

4

ourselves comfortable until Marshal Tibbit gets here? Is that all right by you, mister?"

Fargo reluctantly nodded. Lowering the Colt, he stepped back and twirled it into his holster. "I have coffee left if anyone wants some."

Wilson smiled and nodded. "That would be nice, yes. I'm not used to being up this late. It must be pushing midnight."

Fargo hunkered to rekindle the fire. He kept an eye on Harvey, who had gone over to Dugan and McNee; the three were huddled together, whispering. When the flames were crackling, Fargo turned to Tom Wilson. "You say this woman went missing?"

"She lives in Haven with her mother and father. Works at the dry goods store. They say she went out to hush the dog, which was making a ruckus, and never came back in. When her parents went out they found the dog with its throat slit and poor Myrtle was nowhere to be seen."

"It was a big dog, too," a townsman mentioned. "Whoever killed it had to be awful quick or awful strong or both."

"It wasn't me," Fargo said.

"I don't think it was you, either," Wilson said, "but we'll let the marshal decide what to do with you."

"Could it have been hostiles?" Fargo asked. He was thinking of the Apaches. They had no love for the white man, or white woman.

"If it was, it's the first lick of trouble in a coon's age. We're a fair-sized town and the heathens leave us be."

Harvey, Dugan and McNee came up and the former snapped at Wilson, "Why are you being so friendly? For all we know, he took Myrtle and she's lying out there somewhere strangled to death. This tramp should—"

Fargo had listened to enough. He swept up out of his crouch and slammed his right fist into Harvey's jaw. He didn't hold back. Harvey cried out and staggered but he didn't fall. Fargo set himself and waded in but before he could land another blow Dugan and McNee leaped in, fists flying. Fargo blocked, countered, slipped punches but not all of them. Pain flared in his left cheek, his shoulder, his ribs. He got his left forearm up in time to deflect a looping swing by Dugan and retaliated with lightning jabs that drove Dugan back. McNee sprang in, and again Fargo's ribs complained. A quick hook and Fargo had the satisfaction of pulping McNee's lower lip. For a moment he was clear, but only for a moment. Harvey came at him again. Fargo stood his ground and gave as good as he got. He was so intent on Harvey that he forgot about Dugan and McNee but he was reminded when they flung themselves at his arms.

Fargo strained to break free. He had almost succeeded when Harvey hit him in the gut. He kicked Harvey in the shin and Harvey cocked his fists to hit him again. Succor came from an unexpected source.

"Here now, that's enough!" Tom Wilson cried, and shoved between them. "Three against one. I won't have that."

"Out of my way, damn you," Harvey fumed. He tried to shove Wilson aside but Wilson held his ground.

"Simmer down, will you? The marshal's not going to like that you attacked this man."

"*He* took the first swing!" Harvey exploded, and grabbing Wilson by the shoulders, he pushed Wilson so hard that Wilson sprawled onto his back. There was a thud, and Wilson went limp.

"Tom?" one of the others said. The man rushed over and knelt. He slipped a hand under Wilson's head and drew it back, startled. His palm was smeared red. "Damn. He's bleeding. He hit his head on a rock."

"Is he alive?" asked another.

The man with the blood on his palm felt for a pulse and nodded. "He's just knocked out, is all."

Harvey whirled on Fargo. "It's your fault, you son of a bitch."

"You're the one who pushed him," Fargo said.

"Only because he was trying to defend you." Harvey drew his six-gun. "What do you say, boys? Why wait for the marshal? Let's make him tell us where Myrtle is."

"How do you propose we do that?" asked the man kneeling beside Tom Wilson.

"Easy as pie," Harvey said, and slashed the barrel of his revolver at Fargo's face.

It was called pistol-whipping. Lawmen would pistol-whip drunks and belligerents to subdue them. Sometimes the whipping was so severe that those who were beaten suffered a broken nose and busted teeth and were left black-and-blue for weeks.

Fargo had no intention of letting that happen. As Harvey swung, he ducked, and the pistol flashed over his head. Instantly he brought the heel of his right boot down on the tip of Dugan's left boot. Dugan howled in pain and his grip slackened enough that Fargo swung him bodily at McNee and both went tottering. Harvey was raising his arm to use the pistol. In a streak, Fargo had his Colt out and slammed the barrel against Harvey's face, splitting Harvey's cheek. Harvey forgot himself and clutched at his face; he would have done better to protect his gut.

Fargo drove his left fist in so far, he would have sworn his knuckles brushed Harvey's spine. Harvey buckled at the knees but Dugan and McNee had recovered and hurled themselves at Fargo, seeking to seize his arms as they had before. Fargo clipped Dugan across the head and Dugan toppled. McNee dodged, clawed for a pistol on his left hip, and was so slow unlimbering it that Fargo smashed him twice across the chin.

"Enough!" the man who was next to Tom Wilson cried. "In God's name, stop this!"

Fargo wanted to hit them some more. But both Dugan and McNee were down and Harvey was on his knees, doubled over. He nodded and stepped back.

Suddenly another townsman was behind him and jammed a cocked revolver against the back of his head.

"Hold it right there, mister."

"Danvers, what in hell are you doing?" asked the man kneeling beside Wilson.

"I think Harvey is right. If this hombre was innocent he wouldn't have made such a fuss." Danvers reached around and took Fargo's Colt. "Let go or I'll squeeze this trigger, so help me."

Fargo swore, and let go.

Harvey was struggling to his feet. "Thanks for seeing sense, Danvers," he said. "Now let's revive Dugan and McNee and get to it." He leveled his revolver at Fargo. "Fetch a rope."

Danvers moved toward their horses.

"What are you up to?" demanded the man on his knee. "It can't be what I think it is."

"Shut the hell up," Harvey said. "We're going to do what we should have done when we found this bastard." He grinned a vicious grin. "We're going to hang him."

2

Fargo was furious. With a revolver jammed to the back of his head and another pointed at his face, there was nothing he could do as his arms were seized and his wrists bound behind his back. They brought the Ovaro over and he was boosted onto the stallion.

Harvey took the reins. Dugan and McNee kept their weapons on Fargo as Harvey led the stallion toward the trees on the east side of the clearing. Danvers snatched a burning brand from the fire and held it aloft to light the way.

Tom Wilson still hadn't come around. The last two men stayed with him. They made it plain they wanted no part of the hanging.

"Last chance to tell us what you did with Myrtle," Harvey said.

Fargo had one chance. But for him to succeed he needed to whittle the odds of taking lead. So he lied. "She's in the trees yonder."

Harvey stopped. "What?"

"She's trussed up in the trees to the west," Fargo said. "About ten steps in from the clearing."

"Did you hear that?" Dugan said excitedly. "She's alive!"

"You and McNee go see," Harvey directed. "Be quick about it. We want to get this done before the marshal shows up."

They hustled across the clearing.

Fargo tensed his legs. Danvers was watching the other two run off but Harvey was still holding the reins and looking up at him. He needed Harvey to look away. The next instant Harvey did. Hunching forward, Fargo jabbed his spurs and clamped his legs tight and the Ovaro burst into motion, tearing the reins from Harvey's grasp. Harvey cursed and banged off a shot but by then the Ovaro was in the woods. Fargo bent as low as he could as branches whipped at his face and eyes.

The reins were dangling and he hoped they didn't become snagged.

Behind him Harvey was bellowing for the rest to mount and give chase.

Usually the stallion could outrun most any horse alive. But it was night and the woods were thick and, worse, Fargo couldn't control the stallion with his arms tied. He used his spurs again, his chest nearly flat on the Ovaro's back. His cheek was nicked by a limb. His left shoulder seared with pain.

Fargo leaned to the right and the Ovaro veered in the direction he wanted. He was counting on enough of a quick lead to stay ahead of his pursuers. But when he glanced back they were in hard pursuit and closer than he liked. Revolvers boomed but they were shooting in the dark on moving horses and they were poor shots.

The Ovaro crashed out of the trees onto the road. Instinctively, it turned and raced down it rather than into the woods on the other side.

Fargo tried to hike his leg to get at the Arkansas toothpick in the ankle sheath in his boot but he was afraid of losing his balance so he lowered it again.

His pursuers reached the road and goaded their mounts to greater effort. He used his spurs. The road was straight, thank God, and he held his own. Then a sharp bend hove out of the night and the stallion went around it so fast that Fargo had to cling tight with his legs or be thrown violently off.

Someone was shouting. It sounded like Harvey, yelling for the others to shoot Fargo. A few more shots were sent his way to no effect. Few townsmen or farmers ever practiced daily at shooting. They might plink targets once in a while, and hunt now and then, but that was it.

Another bend, and the Ovaro veered dangerously near the trees. Fargo ducked under a jutting limb and felt it brush his hat. He began to think that maybe—just maybe—he would get away even with his hands tied when another branch loomed. He ducked but it caught him across the chest and lifted him clear and he was slammed to the ground with such force he felt it in his bones. The impact, the pain, dazed him. Dimly, he was aware of pounding hooves and then voices and hands grabbed his arms and the light from the burning brand splashed over him. They hauled him roughly to his feet. His head cleared just as Harvey punched him in the stomach.

"That's for tricking us, you son of a bitch."

Fargo kicked him between the legs.

Bleating in agony, Harvey clutched himself and folded at the waist. He cursed up a storm and staggered, his face dark with rushing blood.

"You bastard," McNee said, and struck Fargo on the jaw, a backhand that didn't hurt much.

"Let's hang him and get this over with," Dugan said.

Danvers had a rope as well as the brand. He waggled it and said, "All we need is the right tree."

Harvey was slow to recover. Glaring at Fargo, he straightened and grinned his vicious grin. "Mister, I'm going to enjoy this. Whether you took Myrtle or not doesn't hardly matter anymore." He snatched the rope from Danvers and rigged a noose. Knocking Fargo's hat off, he slid the noose over Fargo's head and around his neck, and laughed. "Like your new necktie?"

They pushed Fargo toward the woods. He fought, planting a boot on Dugan and shouldering McNee. Before he could spring clear he was brought down by a sweep of Harvey's leg. Dugan and McNee pounced and held him fast.

"Damn, he's a wildcat," Dugan said.

"He'll soon be a dead one," Harvey said.

Danvers pointed with the brand and exclaimed, "Look at this! His horse didn't leave him."

The Ovaro had come back. The stallion walked up to Fargo and Harvey gripped the reins. "Right obliging. Now we can hang him on his own animal and not one of ours."

A tree at the edge of the road suited them. It had a thick limb, easily reached on horseback. Fargo fought but they got him up and on the stallion. Dugan and McNee each held a leg while Harvey climbed on his horse and tossed the other end of the rope over a higher limb.

The noose was so tight Fargo could hardly breathe. He didn't beg or ask them to spare him. He glared and grit his teeth and wished to hell his hands were free so he could show these sons of bitches what he thought of them. He saw Harvey raise a hand to smack the Ovaro.

"I can't wait to see your face turn purple and your tongue bulge out," Harvey crowed.

"Just get it over with," Danvers urged.

That was when hooves pounded, and from the other direction came another group of riders. At the forefront was the townsman who had gone off to fetch the marshal and beside him a dumpling of a man in a brown suit with a badge pinned to his vest.

"Hold on, there!" the lawman shouted. "What do you think you're doing?"

"Oh, hell," Dugan said.

Harvey swore and raised his hand higher.

"Stop!" the lawman bellowed. "I mean it, Harve Stansfield. You hit that horse and I'll by-God see you behind bars."

To Fargo's unbounded relief, Harvey muttered under his breath and lowered his arm.

The other group came to a stop.

"I don't believe this," Marshal Tibbit declared. "Fixing to

hang a man without a trial. What the hell got into all of you?" Tibbit was overweight and pasty-faced and his voice had a squeak to it and squeaked more the higher he raised it. "I asked you a question," he said when no one responded. "You'd better have a good explanation."

"We think he's the one who took Myrtle," Harvey said sullenly.

"So you *hang* him?" Marshal Tibbit took off his hat and wiped a sleeve across his sweaty brow. He had curly gray hair and big ears the hat had partially hid. "I should arrest all of you."

"Ah, Marion," Danvers said.

"Don't 'Ah, Marion' me," Tibbit replied. "I won't stand for shenanigans like this—you hear me?"

Fargo twisted his neck, scraping his skin on the rope as he did. "Cut me down, damn it."

"Whoever you are, I apologize for this," Marshal Tibbit said. "We are normally law abiding. But we have been plagued this past year with god-awful happenings and some of our good citizens have—"

"Cut me down *now*."

"Oh. Certainly." Tibbit gigged his mount next to the Ovaro and reached up and pried at the rope but couldn't loosen it. His nails dug into Fargo worse than the rope.

"Don't you have a knife?"

"A knife?" Tibbit said, acting befuddled. "Why, I think I do." He patted his pockets and produced a folding knife, which he had difficulty opening. He pressed the edge to the rope and cut but the knife was so dull that it took forever for him to slice through a few strands.

"Oh, hell," said a man with the new group. He brought his sorrel up on the other side of the Ovaro and drew a large bone-handled knife from a hip sheath. He was big and brawny and wore a homespun shirt, overalls with suspenders, and a floppy hat. He smelled of cow manure. "Let me, Marshal. You'll be at it a month of Sundays."

13

"Sure, Sam, go ahead," the lawman said sheepishly.

A single slash of Sam's knife and the rope parted above Fargo's head. Another slash and Fargo's wrists were free. Fargo rubbed them, then tore the noose from his neck and threw it to the ground. He brought his knees up on top of the Ovaro and launched himself past Tibbit at Harvey Stansfield. It caught everyone by surprise, Harvey most of all. Fargo slammed into him and smashed him to the ground. He slugged Harvey's jaw, his cheek, his head. Harvey got an arm up but Fargo swatted it aside and punched him twice more. He cocked his arm to do it again and someone gripped his wrist to stop him.

"Enough of that, mister!" Marshal Tibbit said. "I don't blame you for being mad but I can't let you beat him to death."

Some of Fargo's rage faded. Some, but not all. He jerked loose and stood and stepped to Danvers, who recoiled in fear. Fargo held out his hand. "Hand over my Colt."

Danvers fumbled getting it from under his belt and almost dropped it. "Here," he bleated.

Fargo shoved it into his holster. He took several steps back and glared at Dugan and McNee and Danvers and the rest of them. "The next son of a bitch who lays a hand on me, I will shoot dead."

"No need for talk like that," Marshal Tibbit said. "You can't let a little mistake sour you."

"*Little mistake?*" Fargo couldn't believe what he was hearing. He took a stride and jabbed the lawman on his badge. "Some of your good citizens almost hung me. Where I was raised they call that murder. Not a goddamned mistake."

"Of course, of course," Tibbit said, bobbing his double chins. "All I meant was, we can't blow it out of proportion."

Fargo looked at him—really looked at him—and realized that here was a man who had no business wearing that tin star. Overweight and out of shape and with little backbone to boast of, Tibbit was one of those good-natured souls who thought everyone else should be the same and always tried to reason with troublemakers.

"You should listen to yourself sometime," he said.

"How's that again? I hear perfectly fine, thank you. And I should think you'd be more grateful for me saving your life." Tibbit held out his hand. "But what do you say we start over? Where are your things? How about we collect them and take you to town and put you up for the night? To sort of make up for how you were treated."

Fargo stared at the lawman's hand.

"What's the matter? I'm trying to be friendly and mend fences. Can't you meet me halfway?"

"How long have you worn that badge?"

"Why do you ask a thing like that? I've been the town marshal for going on fourteen months. And I do a good job if I do say so my own self." Tibbit chuckled. "But then, Haven is a peaceful little community. Some would call it a stick in the mud with only a bank and a general store and the feed and grain and the houses. But it serves the needs of farmers like Sam, there. Doesn't it, Sam?"

"I can't complain," Sam said.

Fargo grunted. "Peaceful little communities don't go around stringing folks up in the middle of the night."

"I grant you that, yes," Marshal Tibbit allowed. "But Harvey and his friends had cause, of a sort. You see, a local girl has gone missing. The fourth in the past year. So you can't blame them for being rough with you."

"Care to bet?" Fargo said, with a pointed glance at Harvey Stansfield.

"All right. Let's drop that, shall we? What do you say to my invite? Care to partake of Haven's hospitality? I'll even go so far as to put you up at the widow Chatterly's for tonight. She rents out rooms."

One of the townsmen snorted and grinned. "Hell, you can put me up at her place every night of the week. That there is one fine filly."

"You're married," Marshal Tibbit said.

"Married ain't dead, and you'd have to be dead not to admire the widow Chatterly."

"Even if I was dead I would," another man said, and some of them laughed.

"Well?" Tibbit prompted.

Fargo had half a mind to tell them to go to hell. But he wouldn't mind sleeping in a bed for a change, especially if it didn't cost him anything. Plus that talk of the widow had piqued his curiosity. "Does this town of yours have a saloon?"

"As a matter of fact we do," Marshal Tibbit said. "It's called the Leaky Bucket."

Despite all that happened, Fargo chuckled. "That's a new one. I don't suppose it's still open."

"At this hour? I should say not. We're a farming and ranching community, not a rowdy place like Saint Louis." Marshal Tibbit paused and then asked hopefully, "Am I to take it you have decided to accept my offer?"

Fargo nodded.

"Good. You won't regret it, I can promise you."

"We'll see," was all Fargo said.

3

Haven fit its name. The houses had tidy lawns and picket fences. The commercial buildings were well kept. Hitch rails and watering troughs were evenly spaced. The town was so quiet and peaceful that Fargo would have thought he was east of the Mississippi River.

The men left for home and hearth. Harvey rode off with Dugan and McNee after promising to pay the marshal a visit first thing in the morning.

"I aim to give him a piece of my mind about how he treated you," Marshal Tibbit assured Fargo. "He won't do that to anyone else, I can promise."

"Too bad he did it to me."

"Yes, well, Harve has always been a hothead. He acts first and thinks second."

"The other two?"

"McNee and Dugan? They're Harve's friends. Where you find one you usually find them."

"They all family men?"

"Goodness, no. I'm not even sure they like women. Truth is, they spend most of their time at the saloon."

"They work for a living?"

"Oh, they do odd jobs for the farmers and ranchers." Marshal Tibbit glanced at him. "Here now. Why all the questions? You're not thinking of getting back at them, are you?"

Somewhere or other Fargo had heard the expression, "Perish forbid."

"I hope not, for your sake. You might not rate me highly but I take my job seriously. I'll arrest you as quick as look at you if you break the law."

"I noticed you didn't arrest Harvey and his pards."

"Why cause more trouble than there's already been? I believe in restoring the peace and keeping the peace." The marshal drew rein near a gate in a white fence. Dismounting, he opened it. "This is the widow Chatterly's place. Her light is still on, thank goodness. I'd hate to wake her this late."

Flower beds ran along the front of the house. A second-floor window was lit, the shade over it pink. After the lawman knocked a shadow moved across the shade, the shape undeniably hourglass.

Fargo folded his arms. He was sore all over and his neck was smarting.

Harve and those other two had a lot to answer for.

Marshal Tibbit knocked again. "Maybe she won't come down, it being so late and all."

No sooner were the words out of his mouth than the door opened, framing a woman in a floor-length robe. And what a woman, Fargo thought. Lustrous golden hair spilled past slender shoulders. Her face was peaches and cream, her lips strawberries. She had eyes as blue as his and a bosom that needed a lot of robe to cover it.

"Sorry to bother you so late, Helsa," Marshal Tibbit said, taking off his hat. "I'm hoping you can do me a favor."

Helsa Chatterly looked past the lawman at Fargo. "If by favor you mean him, his buckskins look as if he's been rolling around in grass and he has a welt on his jaw. Is he safe to let into my house?"

"I'm perfectly harmless," Fargo answered for himself.

Helsa looked him up and down and said with a slight smile, "I very much doubt that."

"He needs a bed and you're all we've got," Marshal Tibbit said. "One day Haven will have a hotel. Until then . . ."

"Until then my boardinghouse will have to do," Helsa

finished. "Very well. Come on in and I'll show him to his room. But keep it down, if you please. I have another boarder and he retired hours ago."

The inside smelled of flowers, as well it should since there were vases of them everywhere Fargo looked. He tried to walk quietly but his boots thumped on the hardwood floor and his spurs jingled. She led them up a flight of stairs and opened a door at the end of the hall. The room was spotless. A blue quilt covered the bed, and there was a dresser and a night stand.

"Isn't this nice?" Marshal Tibbit said.

"It almost makes up for nearly being hung," Fargo said dryly.

Helsa Chatterly turned. "What was that?"

"The good citizens of your peaceful little community," Fargo quoted the lawman, "tried to treat me to a strangulation jig a while ago."

"What on earth for?" Helsa said to Tibbit.

"Now, now. It's nothing to get excited about. There was a misunderstanding."

"What brought it on, Marion?"

Tibbit looked around as if afraid of being overheard and leaned toward her to whisper, "Myrtle is missing."

"What?" Helsa's hand rose to her throat. "Myrtle Spencer? When did this happen? Why haven't you raised an alarm?"

"I did, my dear," Marshal Tibbit said. "But I raised it quietly. I got together a search party and we went up and down the road but didn't find anyone except this gentleman." He jerked a thumb at Fargo and then said, "Say, you haven't told me who you are."

Fargo gave his name.

"What do you do for a living?" Helsa asked.

"I scout. I track people. I work as a guide. I play cards." Fargo almost added, "I drink a lot."

"A tracker, are you?" Marshal Tibbit said. "That's interesting. Would you be willing to stop by my office tomorrow morning about eight?"

"What for?"

"I'd like to put your skills to use. Maybe you can find Myrtle where the rest of us couldn't."

"I'll think about it," Fargo said. He had no hankering to stay in Haven a minute longer than he needed to. Not after the reception they'd given him.

"You do that," Marshal Tibbit said. "Think about how a young woman's life might depend on how good you can track." He put his hat on and nodded at Helsa and went out.

"He means well," she said.

"Where can I put my horse?"

Around back was a fenced area. Fargo removed the saddle and the saddle blanket and draped them over the top rail. A bay was already there, dozing. He didn't realize Helsa Chatterly was in the doorway watching him until he turned.

"You've never seen anyone take a saddle off?" he joked.

She went into the kitchen and Fargo followed her and closed the door behind him.

"I haven't explained about the few rules I have. Breakfast is at seven sharp. Miss it and you go hungry. I serve light fare around midday if you want any. Supper is at six in the evening and I prefer you let me know in advance if you will be here so I can plan accordingly. There's to be no rowdy behavior. No drinking, for instance. And no loud noise after about ten. You are welcome to sit in the parlor whenever you like, provided you wipe your boots first and don't track in dirt and mud."

"A few rules?" Fargo said.

Helsa smiled. "Perhaps I go a little overboard. You would, too, if you'd seen some of the things my boarders have done. There was one man who put out his cigar by rubbing it against a wall. There was another who snuck whiskey in and got falling-down drunk. Then there was the baritone who fancied he could sing at the top of his lungs any hour of the day or night."

"You've had it rough."

"I know sarcasm when I hear it. But it's not easy being a widow in a town where the men outnumber the women three to one."

"You don't have to stay," Fargo said.

"Yes, I do. I owe it to James. He was my husband." Helsa stopped and stepped to the window and gazed out, her hands clasped in front of her. "A lot of women like to complain about their men, about how worthless they are. I never once complained about James. He was a good man. He came out here on account of me. We lived in Indiana, and I'd heard and read so much about the frontier, I hankered to live out here. James said that whatever I wanted, we would do. That's the kind of man he was."

Fargo could think of another reason the man gave in so easily but he didn't say it.

"So we came west. We got to Prescott and heard about a new town in a beautiful valley. Haven. The Indians left it alone, and the people were peaceful and prosperous. James wasn't sure because it was so far from anywhere but I knew the moment I heard about it that Haven was the place for me."

"You wanted frontier life without the dangers," Fargo said.

Helsa Chatterly turned. "Only a fool courts peril and I flatter myself I'm no fool."

"Go on," Fargo said to mend fences.

"All went well until about a year ago when the first of the young women went missing. Felicity was her name. Her parents were our dearest friends, and James took it hard. He liked her. She was sort of the daughter we never had."

"You didn't have any kids of your own?"

"No, Mr. Fargo. We did not. It's none of your affair but we couldn't. Not for a lack of trying, I might add."

Fargo ran his eyes from the crown of her luxurious hair down over her enticing body to the tips of her small feet. "I bet your husband tried every night, too."

For a second she appeared offended but her face softened

and she said quietly, "The feeling was mutual. I found James very handsome. He had the most piercing blue eyes. A lot like yours. We did it every chance we had."

Fargo gave her charms another scrutiny. He liked earthy women. They didn't put on airs and pretend that "it" was beneath them when secretly they liked "it" as much as most men. "How long has he been dead?"

"I'm getting to that. You see, James tried hard to find out what had happened to Felicity. He would go out at night, late, which wasn't like him, and when I asked where he was going, he wouldn't say. He told me it was best I didn't know but that he had an idea about who had taken her. That surprised me. At the time there was a difference of opinion."

"Difference how?"

"Felicity had gone off for a walk in the middle of the afternoon as she usually did and she didn't return. Some assumed it must have been Apaches. Others thought maybe a bear or a mountain lion got her. Still others that she got lost in the woods and couldn't find her way back. James was convinced a foul misdeed had been committed." Helsa's features clouded. "And then he disappeared, too."

Fargo's interest was growing.

"His horse was found about a mile from Haven with blood on the saddle. But there was no sign of James. Since then three other girls have vanished, which proves he was right about a sinister purpose."

"You stay to honor his memory?"

Helsa smiled. "Something like that, yes. And because I truly do love it here."

"Do you have any notions on who killed him?"

Sadness wiped her smile away. "I wish I did. I wish I knew so the marshal could arrest whoever it is and put them on trial and they could be hung by the neck until they are dead." Helsa's frown deepened. "Everyone in Haven is on tenterhooks. We would all of us like to get to the bottom of the mystery and find the person responsible."

22

"Not everyone," Fargo said.

"Excuse me?"

"Whoever is taking the women doesn't want to be found."

Helsa moved to the hall. "Look at me, talking my head off when it's so late and you probably want to turn in."

"How many folks live here?"

"In the town itself or all together? Counting the farmers and ranchers and their families, I believe the total is one hundred and twelve but I could be mistaken. The assessor would know. Why?"

Fargo did the numbers in his head. She had said there were about three men for every woman. "That makes about seventy to eighty of them men?"

"Over eighty, I believe. So yes, the marshal has a lot of suspects, if that is what you're getting at." Helsa sadly sighed. "It's so frustrating. Two families have left because of the disappearances. Now with Myrtle gone and her dog killed, it wouldn't surprise me if more go."

"Aren't you worried it could happen to you?"

Helsa shook her head. "No. None of the women taken were married. As a widow, I should imagine I'm safe. Whoever is to blame hankers after young unwed girls."

"Or he likes green pastures," Fargo said.

"In what way?"

"Girls are more likely to be virgins."

"What a sick thing to say," Helsa said.

"For some men that's important. Me, I like females with experience." Fargo stared at her bosom.

"Show more respect, if you don't mind. I'm beginning to have second thoughts about letting you stay."

Fargo went over to her. He didn't touch her; he stood so close that he could feel the warmth of her body through the robe and she could feel the warmth of his. "I have plenty of respect. As you said, it's not easy being a woman alone. But a woman alone has the same needs as a woman who isn't. All I'm doing is letting you know I'm interested."

"Well," Helsa said, and blushed. "You come right out with it, don't you? What makes you think I would care?"

Fargo looked at a spot on her robe below the belt.

"I should slap you."

"You won't."

Helsa started down the hall, saying over her shoulder, "There will be no more talk about that, not while you're under my roof. I'm glad I only have to put you up for one night."

Fargo liked how her backside swayed as she walked. "I just might stay longer," he said to himself, and grinned.

4

At quarter past eight Marshal Marion Tibbit came up the street, yawning and scratching himself. His clothes looked as if he had slept in them. His hat was pushed back on his head and he squinted in the glare of the morning sun. A rolled-up newspaper was under one arm. He came under the overhang and groped in his pocket. Producing a key, he inserted it into the lock and was about to turn the latch when he glanced over and gave a start. "Mr. Fargo! My word. I didn't see you leaning there."

Fargo straightened and came out of the shadows. "You said something about wanting my help. And we have things to talk about."

"If you mean the lynching, I consider the matter closed. You may press charges if you so wish but no jury will convict those men, not given the circumstances."

"It's those circumstances I'm interested in."

"Well, then, please, come on in. Would you care for a cup of coffee? I can't start my day without four or five." Tibbit opened the door and went over to a potbellied stove in the corner.

The office was Spartan: a desk, a chair behind the desk and another in front of it, the stove, a small cupboard where the coffee and cups and other things were kept, and a cell for prisoners. At the moment the cell was empty.

Fargo sat in the chair in front of the desk and placed his

left ankle on his right knee. On the desk were a tobacco pouch and a pipe. It explained the odor.

"How was your stay at widow Chatterly's?" Marshal Tibbit asked as he kindled a flame in the stove. "I trust it was pleasant."

"I liked it so much I might stay a few nights more."

"That's fine. Just fine." Tibbit took the lid off the coffeepot and got a pitcher down from the bottom shelf of the cupboard. The pitcher was filled with water. "I hope you don't expect me to pay," he said as he poured. "I agreed to one night and one night only. Any more and you must pay for them yourself."

"That's fair."

"What's your reason for wanting to stay there, if I might ask?"

Fargo pictured the widow's face and lips and bosom, and felt a twinge low down. "I'd like to see the landlady bare-assed naked."

Tibbit's mouth fell open and he started to straighten so fast, he nearly dropped the pitcher. "I trust you are joshing."

"Why?"

"She's not that kind of woman. Helsa is a respectable lady and must be treated as such."

"You don't sleep with many females, do you?"

"What a thing to ask," Tibbit retorted. "I don't see where that's any of your business. But for your information I have slept with my share."

Fargo was willing to bet he could count them on one hand and have fingers left over but he changed the subject. "Last night you mentioned putting my tracking skills to use."

"That's right. I did, didn't I?" Tibbit got the coffee down. "How good a tracker are you?"

There were plenty of veteran army officers and seasoned frontiersmen who would rate him as one of the best but all Fargo said was, "I can trail a buffalo good enough."

"A buffalo?" Marshal Tibbit said, sounding disappointed.

"Why, anyone can do that. They leave tracks as big as pie plates. I need—" He stopped and stared. "Wait a second. You were pulling my leg, weren't you?"

"Might have been," Fargo conceded.

Tibbit chuckled. "It's nice you have a sense of humor. Take that incident with the rope, for instance. Give yourself time and you'll laugh about it."

Fargo thought of Harvey Stansfield and Dugan and McNee, and his neck and face grew warm. "Not in this life."

"What I'd like to do is take you to the Spencer place and let you have a look around. She was only taken last evening so there might still be sign."

"Didn't you look?"

"I did, yes, but it was dark. I used a lantern, which didn't help much." The lawman shrugged. "I freely admit I'm terrible at it. I couldn't track a cow down the middle of Main Street. In my defense, I've never hunted a day in my life so I've never really had to do much tracking."

"What did you do before you pinned on that badge?"

Tibbit came and sat behind the desk. He propped his boots up and laced his fingers behind his head. "Promise not to laugh?" He didn't wait for Fargo to answer. "I was a traveling salesman. I sold ladies' corsets, if you can believe it."

"I can believe it," Fargo said.

"I got tired of always being on the go and always scrabbling to make ends meet. About a year and a half ago I came to Haven. I only intended to stay a couple of days and sell as many corsets as I could and then catch the next stage out. But I liked it here so much that I asked a councilman's wife if she knew of any jobs that were to be had, and as it happened, there was one."

"You went from corset salesman to lawman?"

Tibbit laughed. "I know what you're thinking. What did a seller of ladies' corsets know about the law? I admit I knew little. But my enthusiasm impressed the town council. And as

27

it so happens, I'm a fast reader. I've gone through every law book and statute there is."

"There's more to wearing a tin star than law books."

"I grant you that, yes. But don't you see?" Tibbit spread his hands in delight. "I have a job I love. I have a roof over my head and the roof is my own. No more endless travel. No more having to listen to customers carp about their corsets. I'm in heaven." The gleam of happiness faded from his eyes and he put his boots on the floor. "Or I was until this whole missing women horror started. The first one, I thought for sure the Apaches were to blame. Everyone knows they take white women to their wigwams and have their way with them."

Fargo smothered a laugh. Most Apaches regarded white women as weak and helpless and unable to endure the Apache way of life. Apache warriors would much rather have a woman of their own kind.

Tibbit had gone on. "Then three months later the second woman disappeared, and I wasn't so sure anymore. By the time the third woman went missing after another three-month interval there was no longer any doubt. It had to be a white man."

"Or men," Fargo said.

"Eh? Oh, yes. Possibly."

"Were the women always taken three months apart?"

"Give or take a week or two. Isn't that strange? There must be a reason but it eludes me."

Fargo could see where a lot might elude Marion Tibbit.

"The town council is demanding action and I don't blame them. Those poor women, vanishing into thin air. I would like nothing better than to find them and restore them to their families. But I'm at my wit's end."

"So you clutch at a straw and ask a tracker for help," Fargo said.

"It can't hurt, you taking a look. You don't mind, do you? You'd be doing this community, and me, a great favor. And I did save your life last night, if you'll recall."

"You must have been good at it," Fargo said.

"I beg your pardon?"

"Corset selling. You could talk rings around a tree."

Marshal Tibbit laughed. "I guess I was, at that. I admit I am a talker. On the rare occasions a man gets drunk and rowdy in Haven, I don't drag them here to the cell against their will. I talk them into spending the night of their own free will. I prefer to use my tongue, not my pistol."

"I like to use my tongue, too."

"You do? You could have fooled me. You're rather the laconic type, I've noticed."

"Laconic?"

"Yes. You don't speak unless you have to and even then . . ." Tibbit stopped. "You just did it again, didn't you? Pulled my leg?" He got up and went to the stove and touched the coffeepot. "It shouldn't be long."

"Why haven't you asked for help before this?" Fargo asked.

"From whom? The Rangers? They mainly deal with Indians, and they might disband soon, anyway, I hear. The army? Most of the troops have been recalled east because of the war. The county sheriff? There isn't one because they haven't gotten around to forming a county yet." Tibbit shook his head, and sighed. "No, there's just me."

"And four missing girls."

"And a missing man. Didn't Helsa tell you about her husband?"

"She did."

"That makes five that I know of. I also got a letter six months ago from a woman in Illinois wanting to know if I'd seen her brother, who was supposed to be in this area. I told her I never had."

"The tally is climbing."

"Yes. Worrisome, isn't it? Makes me wonder exactly what I'm up against."

The coffee was soon done. The lawman filled two cups

and filled his with cream and enough sugar to gag a goat. Fargo took his black.

Outside, the street was alive with people moving to and fro. A buckboard clattered past. A man and his family of five were about to go into the general store across the street.

Tibbit had been unusually quiet but now he pointed and asked, "Do you recognize him?"

Fargo looked. "The farmer who cut me down last night."

"Sam Worthington. As fine a gentleman as you'll find anywhere. Notice anything about his family?"

"He has a girl about eighteen."

"She's all of twenty but not married yet. Her name is Melissa. A pretty thing, and smart. She came to me about a week ago, in secret. Said she thought someone was spying on her. I thought maybe whoever took the other girls would try to take her, so I was keeping watch on their farm. And wouldn't you know? It was Myrtle Spencer who disappeared." Tibbit took a sip of his coffee-flavored sugar water. "I'd like to take you out to the Worthington farm after we talk to the Spencers, if you're willing. There's something I'd like you to see."

"Don't get your hopes up," Fargo said. "I'll take a look-see but I can't promise I'll be of any help."

"The fact that you are willing to lend a hand means more to me than you can imagine." Tibbit sounded genuinely grateful. "If you don't mind my asking, what prompted you to agree? Do you possess a strong sense of civic responsibility?"

"No."

"Was it sympathy for the girls who have gone missing and for their families?"

"No."

"You want to help because it's the right thing to do?"

"No."

Tibbit placed his elbows on the desk. "Then why, in heaven's name?"

"Two reasons," Fargo said.

"The first being . . . ?"

"The widow."

Marshal Tibbit bobbed his head as if waiting for Fargo to go on, and when Fargo didn't he said, "Does this have to do with seeing her—how did you put it?—bare-assed naked?"

Fargo nodded. "I need something to keep me busy until I bed her."

Tibbit sat back and uttered a bark of a laugh that died in midbark. "Wait. My God. You're serious. Why, that's outrageous."

"She's a fine-looking female."

"Yes, true, but still," Tibbit sputtered. He opened his mouth to say more but apparently changed his mind and closed it again. He drank some coffee and cleared his throat. "All right. Let's put that aside for the moment. Although I must say, your gall is remarkable. You've only known her one night. Do you honestly think you have a chance?"

"She's a woman and I'm a man."

"It takes more than that."

"No," Fargo said, "it doesn't."

Tibbit fixed Fargo with slightly bewildered look. "All right. What's your second reason?"

"That necktie social last night."

"I don't understand."

"I was nearly hung because some of those men blamed me for the women who have gone missing. I'd like to find the son of a bitch who took those women and show him what I think of having a rope around my neck."

"You're saying you want to help so you can see him hung?"

"I'm saying I want to find him so I can kill the bastard myself."

Marshal Tibbit opened a drawer and took out a half-empty bottle of whiskey. He opened it and poured some into his cup and tilted the cup to his mouth and gulped. It brought on a

31

coughing fit and it was a while before he could say, "You are the most singular person I've ever met."

"I'm no different from anyone else."

"Yes, you are. But I'm afraid I must disappoint you. I can't have you taking the law into your own hands. If we find whoever is responsible, I intend to place him under arrest so he can be tried in a court of law. Under no circumstances will I let you deprive him of due process."

Fargo sat silent.

"I must insist on your word. Promise me that you won't shoot him on sight. I'll have to refuse otherwise, as much as I can use your help."

"I won't shoot on sight," Fargo said.

"Good." Tibbit smiled and drank heartily. "Very good." He set down his cup. "I have to make my morning rounds and then we can be on our way. It shouldn't take more than ten minutes or so. You're welcome to stay here until I get back." Standing, he smoothed his jacket and adjusted his hat and strode out with the air of a rooster on the peck.

Fargo went to the window. The Worthington family came out of the general store and moved down the street. Three riders came up it from the other direction and dismounted in front of the Leaky Bucket. They tied their horses to the hitch rail and filed in.

"Well now," Fargo said. He went out. Staying close to the buildings he came to the saloon and peered in the front window. The three were at the bar.

The only other customer was an older man at a table by himself. Fargo pushed on the batwings. They didn't squeak and no one heard him until he was close enough for his spurs to give him away. Two of the three glanced over their shoulders to see who it was.

"You!" Dugan blurted.

"What are you doing here?" McNee asked.

Harvey Stansfield heard them and put down his glass and turned—straight into Fargo's uppercut.

32

5

The blow smashed Harvey against the bar. Even as it landed Fargo was turning. He punched Dugan on the jaw and sent him stumbling, spun, and unleashed a flurry of jabs and a right cross that McNee tried to counter but couldn't. McNee tottered. Again Fargo whirled. Harvey was clinging to the bar and shaking his head, trying to recover. Fargo rammed a fist into his jaw and Harvey's knees folded. Pain in his side let him know that Dugan had jumped into the fray and he retaliated with a swift straight right to the jaw that rocked Dugan onto his bootheels and then with a looping left. Dugan dropped.

More pain, this time in the small of Fargo's back. Wincing, he turned just as McNee drew back a fist to hit him again. Fargo blocked, sidestepped, planted a solid swing to the face, sidestepped again and planted another. McNee fell against the bar.

Harvey Stansfield was on his knees, still shaking his head. He had yet to land a blow. Fargo struck once, twice, and Harvey sprawled onto his belly, out to the world. Fargo pivoted. Dugan was still down but conscious and struggling to rise to his hands and knees. Fargo kicked him in the head. That left McNee, who thrust out a palm and bleated, "No! Don't!"

Fargo hit him so hard it nearly broke his hand. McNee's eyelids fluttered and he oozed to the floor and was still.

"God in heaven," the bartender said.

Fargo stepped back and surveyed the three limp forms. "When they come to, tell them something for me."

"Anything you want, mister."

"Tell them I went easy on them."

"Jesus."

"Tell them they better have gotten it through their thick heads that they can't go around stringing up whoever they please."

"Oh," the bartender said. "You're him. The one they were bragging about right before you came in."

"They bragged about trying to lynch me?"

The bartender's Adam's apple bobbed. "They were joking and laughing about it and Harvey, there, was saying as how it was a shame the marshal stopped them."

Fargo swore. "Then tell them something else for me. Tell them that the next time I see them I'm going to do this again."

"They won't like that."

"Tell them I'm going to keep on doing it until they leave town, or I do."

"You sure hold a grudge."

"If you had a noose around your neck you would too." Fargo wheeled and stalked toward the batwings, and stopped.

Marshal Tibbit was holding them open, his face more pasty than usual. "I told you to drop it."

"Wishful thinking."

Tibbit nodded at the unconscious forms. "I'll pretend I didn't see that. But I heard what you said. You can't keep beating them up whenever you like."

"You're going to have to pretend a lot more," Fargo said.

"Can't you be reasonable?"

"Were they reasonable last night?"

"Everyone makes mistakes."

Fargo wanted to grab him by the shirt and shake him until his teeth rattled but instead he said, "Stepping on someone's foot in a crowded room is a mistake. Hanging someone by the neck until they are dead is worse."

"I can see it's pointless to try and reason with you." Tibbit stepped back and held a batwing open. "Let's drop it for now and we'll go visit the Spencers. We won't need horses. They live right at the edge of town."

That was fine by Fargo. He could use some air. His blood still roared in his veins.

The house was one of those with a white fence and green grass. It sat farther back than most and was bigger than most, too. It had been painted a shade of yellow.

"Must be hard on the eyes on a bright day."

"What?" Tibbit said. "Oh. Yes. It's my understanding that Francis—that's the wife—is fond of lemons. She has them brought in special at the general store and eats them all the time and always drinks lemon tea. So she had Joseph paint the house so it resembled a lemon." He chuckled. "Don't people do the strangest things?"

"That's one way of putting it," Fargo said.

"What's another?"

"People are damn stupid."

The gate didn't creak and there was a stone path to the porch. Marshal Tibbit knocked and took off his hat. In a minute the door opened. A mouse of a woman in a yellow dress, her eyes bloodshot from crying and her face haggard from lack of sleep, exclaimed, "Marshal!" She grabbed his jacket and asked, "Have you found her? Have you found my Myrtle?"

"No, ma'am, not yet I haven't," Tibbit said, and gently pried her fingers off. "I need to look around again, if you don't mind."

"What good will that do?" Francis Spencer demanded. "She's not here."

"I know that. But I didn't have much of a chance last night and I have a man with me who might be able to help us."

Francis fixed her bloodshot eyes on Fargo. "Him? What good can he do?"

"He's a tracker."

"Tracker?"

"He reads sign as good as an Indian can."

"He almost looks like one, as dark as he is. If it wasn't for that beard . . ." Francis stopped and bowed her head. "I'm sorry, mister. I don't mean to compare you to a redskin. I'm not myself at the moment."

"I've been called a lot worse," Fargo said.

Francis moved aside. "Come in, please, both of you."

"Where's your husband?" Tibbit asked.

"Joseph isn't here. He went off at first light with several men to search for Myrtle. He plans to stay out all day if need be."

"He should have told me."

"Why? Would you have tried to stop him?"

"Of course not."

"He wouldn't let you anyway," Francis said. "It's our daughter we're talking about. You know how devoted he is to her. So am I." Francis's eyes misted and she dabbed at them with her sleeve. "I'm sorry," she apologized again. "I can't seem to keep from crying."

"It's to be expected," Tibbit said, kindly. "Why don't you show us out back and we will take it from there?"

The backyard had an outhouse, a small pen for horses, and a chicken coop. The ground was mostly grass. To one side a stake and a rope showed where the dog had been tied. A mound of fresh earth showed where the dog was now.

"Tell me again how it happened," Fargo requested.

"There's very little to go on. The family was in the parlor and heard their dog bark. When it didn't stop, Myrtle came out to shush it. That was the last they saw of her."

"Why didn't the father or mother come out?"

Tibbit shrugged. "Why should they? The dog was Myrtle's. She'd raised it from a pup and it went with her everywhere."

"The parents didn't hear anything? No shouts or screams or a scuffle?"

"Not a sound. Joseph said that the barking stopped as soon as Myrtle went outside. He went on reading and Francis went on sewing until it occurred to them that Myrtle had been gone an awful long time. Joseph went out and that's when he saw the dog with its throat cut."

Fargo went to the rope and stake. The dog's constant pacing had worn a lot of the grass away. Its big prints were everywhere. "What kind was it?"

"Kind?" Tibbit said, and shrugged. "A mongrel. Big as a calf."

"You said its throat was cut."

"Yes. So?"

"So why did it let the killer get close? Did the killer sneak up on it? Or was there something else?"

Tibbit said excitedly, "As in, maybe the dog knew the killer? I hadn't thought of that."

"If it knew the killer why did it bark?"

"Oh. Damn." Tibbit rubbed his double chins. "This law business can try a man's brain."

Fargo examined the tracks closest to the rope. Most were the dog's. A small foot with a petite shoe he figured to be Myrtle's. There was also a number of tracks made by the same man—store-bought shoes with wide heels. "Does the father wear shoes or boots?"

"Joseph?" Tibbit did more rubbing. "I believe he wears shoes. He's the town butcher and has no real need for boots. Why?"

"His tracks," Fargo said, and moved to a lone print on the other side of the stake. The toes pointed toward the stake, which meant whoever made it had come over the fence and, if the dog was facing the house, come up behind it. He sank to a knee and examined the print closely.

"What do you have there?"

"How many people were in the backyard last night?"

"Let's see." Tibbit ticked them off on his fingers. "There were Joseph and Francis, of course. There was me, when I got here. And a couple of townsmen. Oh, and Sam Worthington."

"No one else?"

"No. I shooed everybody out except for Joe and his wife and told them not to let anyone else in as a precaution in case there was a clue that might be disturbed. Do you think I did right?"

"Know anyone who wears a boot with a split heel on the left foot?"

"How would I know that? I don't go around asking folks to lift up their feet."

"Maybe you should start." Fargo walked to the back gate. He opened it and noticed that unlike the front gate, it squeaked. Bare dirt was on either side, covered with tracks from the family's comings and goings. At the edge of the grass was another footprint with a split heel. He closed the gate and roved the yard. The chickens were out and moved out of his way, clucking in annoyance. The rooster flapped its wings. It gave him a thought. "Were the chickens acting up or just the dog?"

"I never thought to ask. Who cares about chickens?"

In the pen were two sorrels, older horses, well broke to the saddle, if Fargo was any judge.

Tibbit had followed him over. "The smaller one is Myrtle's. The other Francis usually rides. And no, before you ask, I don't know if they were acting up, either."

Fargo checked the ground around the pen. He didn't find any of the split-heel tracks. He walked back to the gate and gazed past it at a field of tall grass and wildflowers that bordered a thick forest. Going out, he started across the field, Tibbit sticking to him like a burr. Trampled grass and crushed flowers caused Fargo to grunt.

"What?"

"This is the way they went."

"They?"

"Whoever took Myrtle was carrying her."

"How do you know?"

"If two people were running side by side there would be more grass trampled. The girl was either trussed and gagged or he knocked her out."

"How do you know that?"

"Did anyone hear her scream?"

"Oh. No. I see what you're saying." Tibbit coughed. "You're good at this. You should wear a badge yourself."

"Any ten-year-old Apache could do what I'm doing." Fargo followed the flattened vegetation to the trees. A few yards in he squatted and pointed. "Here's where his horse waited. He had this planned out, whoever he was." Fargo reconstructed the abduction in his head. "He went up to the back gate and let the dog see him so it would bark. Then he snuck around the fence. When Myrtle came out and told the dog to hush, he hopped the fence, slit the dog's throat, and jumped her before she could cry out."

"You got all that from the tracks?"

"Some. Some of it I'm guessing."

"That poor girl."

"Either he gagged her or he knocked her out and carried her here and threw her over the horse. Odds are he was long gone before her parents came out to find why she was taking so long."

"Clever rascal," Tibbit said.

"Clever bastard," Fargo amended.

"By now he could be anywhere."

"But he made a mistake."

"He did?"

"He brought the horse close so he wouldn't have to carry Myrtle all that far." Fargo tapped a finger on one of the tracks. "All we have to do is follow these to his lair."

"My word!" Tibbit exclaimed. "That's right. What are you waiting for? Every moment counts."

"On foot it could take days," Fargo mentioned. "We'll collect our horses and do it right."

"Yes. What was I thinking?" Marshal Tibbit happily rubbed his hands together. "This is marvelous. At last I can put an end to the disappearances. Folks won't think so poorly of me."

"And no more girls will be taken."

"Yes, that too." Tibbit turned. "Let's hurry. Maybe we can end this before the sun goes down."

"Provided he doesn't see us coming," Fargo said.

6

Myrtle Spencer's abductor was clever. The tracks wound among the trees like the twisting of a snake, not to make it harder to trail him, since the tracks were fresh and plain, but to slow the trackers down. For over a mile the serpent in the saddle hadn't ridden in a straight line for more than twenty feet. For Fargo it was tedious and slow, constantly having to rein right and left.

Marshal Tibbit wasn't accustomed to so much riding. He complained that his backside hurt and a little later complained that his legs hurt and a little later yet complained that he was sweating all over and could dearly use a hot bath.

"Don't you mean a cold one?"

"No, I always take hot baths. I have delicate skin and cold baths are too rough on me."

Fargo glanced at him.

"What?"

"Nothing."

The forest ended at the brink of a high canyon wall. Fargo drew rein and scanned the bottom but saw no tracks. He reined to the east but there were none along the rim in that direction, so he reined to the west only to find there were none in that direction, either. "What the hell?"

"What's wrong?"

"His horse sprouted wings and took to the air."

"Your jokes are weak," Tibbit said.

Fargo returned to where the tracks came out of the trees.

Below was a talus slope. Made up of loose dirt and small stones, it would give way under the weight of a horse and turn the stones and dirt into a deadly avalanche. The talus was undisturbed—not a single pockmark anywhere. "Stranger and stranger."

"Are you saying we've lost them?"

"The tracks have disappeared into thin air."

"How is that possible?"

"It's not." Fargo racked his brain for an explanation. "Maybe he stopped and wrapped the hooves in hide." But even then, there should have been impressions where the soil was soft. Horses were heavy.

"Well, we got this far at least," Tibbit said. "We've learned that it's one man and he must know the Spencer family really well."

"Caught on, did you?"

"I'm not completely worthless, Mr. Fargo. Whoever this fellow is, he wanted Myrtle and only Myrtle. He had to know the dog was hers, and that if it raised a ruckus she would likely be the one to come out and quiet it." Tibbit pushed his hat back on his head and mopped his brow. "Which doesn't really help much since I'd already come to suspect it must be someone in Haven and not an outsider."

"How did that come to you?"

"Am I to believe a stranger has a cabin off in the mountains somewhere and only comes to town every three months to steal women? What about the rest of the time? He'd need food and other supplies, and Haven is the only place to get them for hundreds of miles around."

"It has to be one of your good citizens," Fargo agreed.

Tibbit frowned. "You won't ever stop needling me about that, will you? Very well. Yes, it has to be one of our good citizens."

Fargo climbed back on the Ovaro and once again reined to the east. This time he went twice as far and when he didn't find any sign of the abductor he wheeled the Ovaro and went to the west twice as far. Once again, nothing. Drawing rein, he leaned on the saddle horn and vented his frustration with a heartfelt, "Damn it to hell."

"I know bad news when I hear it."

"We've lost him," Fargo confirmed. He couldn't remember the last time something like this had happened.

"You tried your best."

"Don't," Fargo said angrily. He reined around and debated whether to try again or make a wide sweep. He chose the latter and gigged the Ovaro into the forest.

Marshal Tibbit brought his mount up next to the stallion. "I'm afraid I can't stay much longer. I have other duties I must attend to. Do you mind searching by yourself for a while?"

"Do what you have to," Fargo said. He'd never had a problem with being alone. Some people did. Some considered it downright unsocial not to crave human company. They liked to live in towns and cities where they were surrounded by others just like them. Not him. He could go weeks or months and not see another living soul and be perfectly content. It seemed to him that just as some depended on liquor to get through the day and others frequented opium dens because they couldn't do without, there were those who couldn't do without people.

Tibbit was trotting off. He smiled and waved and hollered, "Come to my office when you're done."

Fargo squinted skyward. He had hours yet of daylight left, plenty of time to find out how he had been tricked. He rode in a half circle that brought him back to the rim about the same distance to the west of the talus. Nothing. He tried again, a wider loop, searching bent low to better see the ground. Once again, nothing.

Fargo drew rein and put his hands on the saddle horn. "This doesn't make any kind of sense," he said to the Ovaro. There was nothing for it but to try a third time and range wider than ever. He reined into the trees and was soon fifty yards in. Then a hundred. He thought he saw a track and practically swung onto the side of the stallion to be sure— just as a rifle boomed and a pine next to the stallion thudded to the impact of a slug.

The shot came from the direction of the canyon.

Instantly, Fargo reined away and used his spurs. He stayed low over the saddle horn in case the bushwhacker tried again. When he had gone far enough to deem it to be safe, he reined up, vaulted down, and shucked the Henry from the saddle scabbard. Levering a round into the chamber, he stalked toward where he expected the shooter to be—near the rim. But either he was mistaken or the assassin had changed position because he came to the brink without seeing anyone.

Fargo hunkered behind a pine. He figured that whoever was out there would try again if he showed himself. Taking a breath, he stepped into the open. Every instinct he possessed screamed at him not to. He was alert for movement, for the slightest sound.

The woods stayed still.

Fargo stalked to the canyon's edge, stopping often to probe the vegetation. He gazed down at the talus, and lower. No one, nor a mount, was anywhere to be seen. He kicked at the ground and a few pebbles slid over the side. Careful not to silhouette himself, he prowled the rim in both directions.

Half an hour later he was as baffled as he had ever been.

Fargo sat on a boulder to think. Shots didn't come out of nowhere, so where had the shooter been? He was mulling the riddle when he caught the thud of hooves. Not from the canyon, but from toward Haven. Crouching, he crept through the woods until he saw who it was. Waiting until the man was almost on top of him, Fargo stepped out and leveled the Henry.

"Hold it right there."

The big farmer Sam Worthington drew rein. He didn't act the least bit rattled but smiled and said, "Good to see you again, mister."

"What are you doing here?" Fargo couldn't keep the suspicion out of his voice.

"Marshal Tibbit sent me." Worthington patted the animal he was riding. "This is his horse. I was in town with my family and he came up and said as how you were out here alone looking for whoever took Myrtle and he'd feel better if you had someone to watch your back."

That sounded like something Tibbit would do. Fargo lowered the Henry. "Seen any sign of anyone?"

"Besides you?" The farmer shook his head. "Not many folks come out this way except a few hunters now and then."

"Do you know the area pretty well?" Fargo thought to ask.

"Fair, I'd say," Worthington replied. "Me and mine mainly eat beef and chicken but now and then I get a hankering for venison so I've roamed these parts some. Why?"

"Come with me." Fargo climbed on the Ovaro and led the farmer to the canyon. "Ever been down there?"

"Clear at the bottom? I sure haven't. Far as I know, there isn't a way down. Not on a horse, anyhow."

"But you've never really tried."

"No, I haven't. Never had any need. Why? Are you trying to figure out where Myrtle got to?"

Fargo nodded.

"You ask me, it's a townsman. None of the farmers or ranchers would do so terrible a thing."

"Know all of them well?"

"Only a few," Worthington admitted.

"Then you can't really say."

"No. But when you work with the soil day in and day out it gives you a respect for life. Plus all the farmers hereabouts are family men. Quite a few, like me, have daughters. A father would never be so vile as to abduct one."

Fargo wasn't convinced. He'd witnessed more than his share of the unsavory side of human nature, enough to know not to take anyone for granted. "Let's head for town."

"I came all this way for nothing?" Worthington chuckled. "That Tibbit. I like him, you understand, but he's not cut out for the law business."

"To hear him tell it, he's done fine except for the missing girls."

"It's easy to be a lawman when no one ever breaks the law," Worthington said. "Haven is plumb peaceable. No shootings, no knifings or fights." He paused, and grinned. "Not until you came to town, anyhow. The most Tibbit ever has to do is shoo a pig off the street or once in a blue moon have a drunk sleep it off in his jail. The rest of the time he sits in his office with his boots on his desk and takes naps or reads or stuffs himself."

"You must have talked to others about the missing girls," Fargo said. "Doesn't anyone have any ideas?"

"Mister, we have talked ourselves hoarse. Every time one goes missing, it's all we talk about for weeks."

"I take it everyone would like to see whoever is to blame be caught?"

"That goes without saying. I ever catch the bastard . . ." Worthington held out a big hand and closed it tight, his knuckles crackling like walnut shells under a nutcracker.

The farmer was a talker. The rest of the ride, he related to Fargo about how irrigation was the key to raising crops and how the soil wasn't the most fertile in the world but it sufficed and how much he loved working the land and seeing things grow and selling the harvest.

"Farm life is the only life for me." Worthington ended his recital. "My pa was a farmer and his pa before him. It's in the Worthington blood."

Ahead spread the field and beyond it the buildings. Fargo was looking forward to a visit to the saloon. He would treat himself to a bottle of whiskey and a game of cards. Or maybe he would pay the widow Chatterly a visit. He smiled, only to have it turn into a scowl as three figures with drawn six-guns separated from the last of the trees and blocked their way.

"Hold on there," Worthington said, drawing rein. "What's this about?"

"He knows," Harvey Stansfield said with a curt nod at Fargo.

Dugan nodded. "Thinks he can thump us and get away with it. In broad daylight in the saloon, no less."

"I heard about that," the farmer said.

McNee pointed his revolver at Fargo's chest. "No one does that to us. Not ever."

"Ten-year-olds," Fargo said.

Harvey came close to the Ovaro. "You walloped us good this morning, mister. Now it's our turn. Climb down. Do it real slow or we'll blow you to kingdom come." He glanced at Worthington. "You stay out of this, Sam. It's between the scout and us."

"Marshal Tibbit won't like it."

"As if we care what that lunkhead likes or doesn't. The bartender told us that Tibbit stood and watched Fargo, here, tear into us, yet he didn't lift a finger to stop it."

"The law dog will get his one day," McNee vowed.

Fargo's right hand held the reins. His left was on his hip. He started to inch his right toward his holster and Dugan took a long stride and jammed the muzzle of a Smith & Wesson against his knee.

"Go ahead and try but you'll be using a cane the rest of your days."

Harvey Stansfield said, "Look at him, boys. Sitting that saddle so calm and peaceable. He doesn't suspect what we have in store."

"You're not fixing to shoot him, are you?" Worthington asked. "I won't have any truck with killing."

"As much as I'd love to blow out his wick, he's not worth going to prison for, or worse," Harvey said. "We aim to give him what he gave us, is all." He wagged his revolver and said to Fargo, "Get off that pinto."

"It's an Ovaro."

"What's the difference?"

"The markings."

Harvey swore. "Quit your damn stalling and get down. I won't say it again."

Dugan bared his teeth. "I can't wait to start pounding on you, mister. By the time we're done half your ribs will be stove in."

"And most of your front teeth," McNee added.

Fargo put his hands on the saddle horn and slid his boot from the stirrup. He slowly swung his leg over and down. The stallion was now between him and Dugan and McNee.

"About time," Harvey snapped. He glanced toward his friends. "Who wants to start the dance?"

"I do," Fargo said, and sprang.

7

Skye Fargo wasn't an ice-in-his-veins killer. He didn't go around shooting people unless they were trying to shoot him. Harvey, Dugan and McNee—the three jackasses, as Fargo was starting to think of them—had made it plain they intended to stomp him into the dirt. That was why he leaped at Harvey with his fists flying instead of resorting to his Colt and blowing all three to hell.

Fargo slammed his fist into Harvey's jaw and Harvey tottered. Fargo went after him; he swatted Harvey's gun arm and punched Harvey in the gut and in the face. Sputtering and wheezing, Harvey sank to his knees. Fargo whirled and slipped close to the Ovaro as McNee and Dugan came running to help Harvey.

McNee was looking past the Ovaro and never saw Fargo or the cross to the jaw that pitched him facedown in the grass. Dugan was running so fast that he tripped over McNee, squawked like a startled hen, and fell on top of him.

Fargo drew his Colt. He slammed it down hard on the back of Dugan's skull as Dugan sought to rise, then smashed it against McNee's temple as McNee tried to push Dugan off. That left Harvey, who was still holding his stomach and taking great gulps of air. Fargo stepped over to him and Harvey looked up.

"Not again."

"You are one stupid son of a bitch," Fargo said, and whipped the Colt up and in. The thud was music to his ears.

He poked all three with his boot to be sure they were out cold and then slid the Colt into his holster.

"Damn, that was slick," Sam Worthington complimented him. "You're the quickest hombre I ever did see."

"If I had any sense I would shoot them," Fargo said, more to himself than to the farmer.

"It ain't in you though, is it?"

Fargo shook his head.

"Didn't think so. I can usually tell about hardcases. They have a look about them. Or an air, if you want."

"Do they?" Fargo had met some who would smile and shake a person's hand while putting a slug into them with the other.

"You agreed to help the marshal. That right there shows me you're a good man."

Fargo didn't tell him about the widow Chatterly.

"What do you want us to do with them? Haul them to Tibbit so he can toss them in the hoosegow?"

"We'll leave them where they are." Fargo stepped from one to the other, scooped up their revolvers, and stuck the six-shooters in his saddlebags. Forking leather, he reined toward Haven.

"Yes, sir," Worthington said, chuckling. "I can't wait to tell about this. Most everyone will have a good laugh."

It was at the saloon hitch rail that Fargo drew rein. Worthington, stopped, too.

"I'd best get this horse back to Tibbit and collect my family. It's a long ride in the buckboard back to our farm and I'd like to get there before sunset."

The remark pricked Fargo's recollection. "The marshal said something about your daughter thinking she was being watched."

"So Melissa claimed. Now mind, she's my daughter and she's as honest as the year is long, but I can't say I entirely believe her."

"Why not?"

"Melissa came in one day from milking the cows and told us she thought someone had been spying on her. She didn't see anyone. She just felt as if eyes were on her. That went on for more than two weeks. Not every day, but enough that it began to wear on our nerves."

"You thought she was making it up?"

"Of course not. But I never saw anyone, and I tried hard to spot whoever it was. When she went to milk or when she went riding, I'd trail after her, and I never saw a soul."

"Maybe whoever was watching her was too smart for you."

"Could be, I suppose. Or maybe every girl in Haven knew it was about time for the Ghoul to strike again and they were nervous about it."

"The Ghoul?"

"Haven't you heard? That's what some of us have taken to calling whoever is behind this. Marshal Tibbit hates the name and won't ever use it. He says it just scares folks more."

Fargo said, "I'd like to come out to your place and look around for sign."

"Fine by me. In fact, why don't we have you over to supper tomorrow? I promise you my Martha will cook a meal you won't soon forget. And I have cigars if you're a smoking man."

"What time?"

"Say about six? Take the north road out of town and follow it about three miles. We're the last farm you'll come to. You'll know it by the swing on the tree out front and the purple curtains in the windows."

"Six it is." Fargo watched the big farmer ride off down the street and turned and went up the steps and pushed on the batwings. More men were there than last time. He crossed to the bar and thumped it. "Your best whiskey and I don't need a glass."

"I should warn you," the bartender said as he took a bottle from a shelf. "Harve and his two friends are looking for you."

51

"They found me." Fargo opened the bottle and chugged. He smiled as a familiar burning sensation spread from his throat down to his stomach. "Ahhh," he said, and smacked his lips in satisfaction. He glanced at the clock on the wall, fished in his pocket for the coins he needed, and paid and walked out. Unwrapping the Ovaro's reins, he walked down the street, drinking as he went. He hadn't gone a block when a bowl of pudding in a suit came hustling up.

"I wish you wouldn't do that right out on Main Street," Marshal Tibbit said. "It sets a bad example."

"I'm thirsty."

"Even so. There is an ordinance against it, too. I must insist or people will think I can't do my job."

Fargo noticed a number of townsfolk staring. "Hell," he said, and slipped the bottle into his saddlebags for the time being.

"Sam Worthington just told me about your latest run-in with those three troublemakers," Tibbit said. "If you're willing to press charges, I'll arrest them for disturbing the peace."

"No." Fargo continued walking.

"Why not? Do you like that they constantly harass you?"

"I like beating on them," Fargo said.

"One of these times it could turn serious."

"You have an undertaker in this town?"

"As a matter of fact, we do. He also runs the feed and grain and—" Tibbit stopped. "I don't like talk like that. I don't like it even a little bit."

"Then maybe you should put the fear of being stupid into them," Fargo suggested, and ran his tongue over his dry lips.

"I would just as soon they leave town but they haven't done anything that would justify me in running them off."

"Trying to hang a man doesn't count?"

"They got carried away."

"You try my patience, Marshal."

"I don't mean to. I am just being me."

"Be you somewhere else."

52

"Excuse me?"

"Make a nuisance of your worthless self somewhere I'm not."

"That's harsh." Tibbit sounded hurt. "I try to do what's right."

Fargo stopped and stared at him.

The lawman grew red in the face. "Now see here. I invited you to stay and help me, and I won't put up with this treatment."

"Yes," Fargo said. "You will."

Tibbit's lips pinched together and he wheeled and stalked off. He was so mad his body jiggled.

Fargo walked on to the boardinghouse. He tied the Ovaro and took the bottle from his saddlebags. After a long swallow he went up the steps and entered without knocking. He ascended to his room, sat in the chair, and tipped the bottle to his mouth. He was on his fourth tip when there came a light rap on the door.

"Mr. Fargo? I thought I heard you come in?"

"You did," Fargo said.

"Are you decent?"

"I have clothes on."

Helsa Chatterly was smiling when she opened the door but her smile promptly died. "Is that a bottle I see?"

"'Pure Old Bourbon Whiskey,'" Fargo quoted the label, and held the bottle out to her. "Care for a swig?"

"I thought I made my rules plain. One of them is that there is to be no drinking under my roof. None whatsoever," she stressed.

Fargo shook the bottle. "You can break your rule this once."

"No, I can't. A rule is a rule."

"And a thirst is a thirst." Fargo heaved out of the chair and walked over and pressed the bottle to her hand. "I won't tell anyone."

"You are arrogant, sir," Helsa declared.

"What I am is tired from riding around most of the day looking for Myrtle Spencer. My neck is still sore from where the good citizens of this town tried to hang me. I have aches from the fights I've had with three simpletons and I'm mad that someone took a shot at me today and I needed a drink." Fargo waggled the bottle. "Last chance."

"You've been through all that?" Helsa looked at the bottle and then into his eyes. Her own narrowed and she tilted her head as if she were trying to peer into his innermost core. Her luscious lips quirked in a grin and she shrugged. "A swallow can't hurt, I reckon."

Fargo noticed that she didn't wipe the bottle on her sleeve or cough after she gave the bottle back. "You've done that before."

"I'm human," Helsa said.

"You put on a good act."

"I have to. You seem to forget I'm a woman living alone. A widow, no less. Some men seem to take it for granted I'm available. I must be firm to discourage them."

"Here's to firmness," Fargo said, staring at her bosom, and swallowed.

Helsa started to laugh but caught herself. "Honestly, now. Just because I've confided in you doesn't give you an excuse to talk that way."

"What way?"

Ignoring the question, Helsa said, "You have me so flustered I forgot why I came up. Supper is almost ready if you're hungry. I'm afraid it's only beef stew but it's filling."

"I'll wash up and be right down."

Helsa turned to go and stopped in the doorway. "Leave the bottle up here, if you would be so kind."

Fargo set it on the dresser. He filled the wash basin from a pitcher. A cloth and a towel had been provided, and he dipped the cloth in until it was soaked and washed his face and neck and took off his hat and ran his wet fingers through his hair. He toweled and put his hat back on and looked at his reflection in the oval mirror. "Play your cards right and maybe you will win the jackpot."

A grandfather clock was ticking loudly in the parlor. The kitchen table had been set for two, and Helsa was at the stove.

Fargo pulled out a chair and sat. He hung his hat from the back of the chair and clasped his hands in front of him. "Where's your other boarder?"

"He won't be with us. He sells farm implements and he's staying the night with the Ringwalds. He just sold them a cultivator or some such." Helsa opened a drawer and took out a ladle and began ladling stew from a large pot into a china bowl.

"So it's just the two of us."

Helsa looked over her shoulder. "The two of us," she echoed.

Silverware had been set out and there was a cup and saucer and a napkin. Fargo saw a coffeepot on a burner and smelled the rich aroma.

"Here you go." Helsa brought the bowl over, carrying it carefully as it was filled to the brim. She set it down in front of him and in quick order brought a small plate with slices of bread, a butter dish, and salt and pepper. "Try the stew and tell me what you think."

Fargo picked up a spoon and stirred. Chunks of meat had been mixed with carrots, peas and potatoes in a thick sauce. He spooned some into his mouth and slowly chewed. "Delicious."

"There's not too much salt? I like a lot, myself, and sometimes my boarders say I use too much."

Fargo ran his gaze from her lustrous hair to her shapely thighs. "I like salty things."

Helsa coughed and turned to the stove. She brought back the pot and filled his cup with steaming coffee. "I have sugar and cream if you'd like."

"Black is fine." Fargo picked up a butter knife and smeared

a slice of bread thick with butter and dipped it in the stew. It melted in his mouth. He held off on the coffee until after his third bowl. Raising the cup, he sipped. "You make a fine feed, Mrs. Chatterly."

"Call me Helsa. I thank you for the compliment."

"Your food is almost as fine as you are."

"Please, Mr. Fargo."

"Please what? Don't say you would turn any man's head? Don't say I would like to invite you up to my room to finish that bottle together?"

Helsa Chatterly pursed her ruby lips and tapped her red fingernails on the table. "What am I to do with you?"

"Anything you want."

"I'm a lady."

"Ladies have wants too."

"You can't prove that by me."

8

Fargo was about to say that he thought he could when someone knocked on the front door.

"I wonder who that can be. I'm not expecting visitors." Helsa moved past him. "Excuse me a moment."

Fargo grunted and drained his coffee cup. He hoped it wasn't the farm-implement salesman. He got up to refill his cup and was by the stove when Helsa returned. She wasn't alone.

The woman behind her gave the impression of being older than her years. Gray streaked her limp hair and she walked with a stoop yet she had few wrinkles and her eyes, although pools of sorrow, were those of someone half her age. She wore homespun and old shoes and she nervously wrung her hands.

"Mr. Fargo, I'd like you to meet Mrs. Griffith. Susannah Griffith. She very much would like to talk to you."

"I'm listening."

"Go ahead," Helsa urged when the other woman hesitated.

"If you don't mind," Susannah Griffith responded, "I'd like to talk to him in private."

"Oh. Naturally. How remiss of me." Helsa backed from the kitchen, saying, "I'll be in the parlor knitting when you're done."

Susannah Griffith stood watching until Helsa was out of sight; then she came around the table and over to the stove and lowered her voice. "I apologize for coming to see you out of the blue."

To Fargo it hardly mattered. "What can I do for you, ma'am?"

"Is it true you're working with Marshal Tibbit to try and find the monster who is taking our women? The Ghoul?"

"Word spreads fast in a town this size."

"I don't live in town, I live on a farm outside it." Susannah glanced at the hall. "Does the name Griffith mean anything to you?"

"Can't say as it does, no."

"You would think that marshal of ours would have told you." Susannah muttered under her breath, then revealed, "My daughter was the second to disappear. Tamar, her name is. Or was, since I fear she's long since dead."

"I'm sorry to hear that," Fargo said to be polite.

"Almost nine months ago, it was. Hard to believe, the time flies so fast, but Tamar is all I think of, each and every minute of every day. I can't get her out of my head."

"That's to be expected," Fargo said, although he felt nine months was a long time to drown in grief.

"My husband and I hardly talk anymore. He took to the bottle, after, and hasn't come out since. Most nights, like this one, he drinks himself into a stupor early and I have to put him to bed."

"You still haven't said what I can do for you."

Susannah Griffith looked toward the hall. Then, to Fargo's surprise, she unbuttoned the front of her dress and slipped a hand in and pulled out a leather purse. Jingling it, she said, "This is why I've come."

"I don't savvy," Fargo confessed.

"There's eighty dollars in here. All I have in the world. I'm offering it to you as payment."

"For what?"

"I've been told you are a seasoned scout, and tough as rawhide. It could be that you'll succeed where our feeble excuse for a lawman has so spectacularly failed. It could be you'll catch whoever took my sweet Tamar."

"I still don't savvy what you want for your money."

"It's simple." Susannah swiped at a gray bang and whispered, "I don't want you to bring him in alive."

"Ma'am?"

"Do I have to spell it out? If you catch him, kill him. Come see me after the deed is done and the eighty dollars is yours."

All the years Fargo had been playing poker paid off; he didn't let his emotions show. "You hate him that much?"

Susannah Griffith's face contorted like a bobcat's about to rend prey to the bone. "I hate him more than I hate anything. He took my Tamar. I'd kill him myself if I knew who it was. This way, you do it for both of us and no one is the wiser."

"Except me."

"Are you saying you have scruples?"

"I'm saying that if he's unarmed or gives up or throws himself at my feet and begs me to spare him, I can't earn your money."

Susannah thought she understood. "In that case all you have to do is provoke him and claim it was self-defense. No one will hold it against you, and since it will be your word against his, no one can prove otherwise."

"More good citizens than I know what to do with," Fargo said.

"Will you or won't you?"

"I will if I have to."

"That's not good enough. Yes or no?" Susannah demanded. When Fargo didn't answer she grabbed his hand and shoved the purse in it. "Take the money now if that's what it will take to persuade you. I want him dead, you hear me? I want him dead like my Tamar is dead."

Fargo tried to give the purse back but she pushed it away.

"Listen," Susannah said, and leaned in so that her lips practically brushed his ear. "I know something no one else does. Something I've never told my husband or the marshal. Something that might help you."

"Why tell me and not anyone else?"

"Because it would drive my husband deeper into the bottle and I can't trust Tibbit not to let the secret out." Susannah bit her bottom lip. "It's not the kind of thing you want to get around. It's about Tamar. She—" Susannah stopped and closed her eyes and trembled as if she were cold, or deathly afraid.

"Here," Fargo said. He guided her to a chair and eased her down. "Anything I can get you? Coffee? Water?"

"No." Susannah bowed her head. "God, this is hard. I've kept it in so long and here I am confiding in a stranger." She gripped his wrist, her nails digging deep. "I want your word. I want your solemn promise that this will be between you and me and no one else."

"You have it." Fargo had to admit he would like to learn what had upset her so deeply.

"My Tamar. She was the sweetest girl you'd ever want to meet but she wasn't—" Susannah groaned, took a deep breath, and said in a rush, "She wasn't pure."

"Pure?"

"You know."

The revelation tore one of Fargo's earlier hunches to shreds. He sat down across from her. "Your daughter slept around?"

Susannah's head snapped up and she looked ready to bite him. "Goodness gracious, no. What do you take her for? What do you take *me* for? She didn't sleep with a lot of men. Only one. She was in love, or thought she was. I caught her sneaking out one night and threatened to tell her pa if she didn't tell me where she was off to." Susannah put a hand over her eyes and her shoulders slumped. "I figured she was traipsing off to see one of the neighbor boys. But it was worse than that. A lot worse."

"She was going to see a girl?"

Again Susannah's head snapped up. "God Almighty, the things that come out of your mouth."

"Then what?" Fargo asked. The answer hit him even as he asked the question.

"She was going to meet a man. A *married* man."

Fargo stared.

"That's right. My precious Tamar took up with a man who had a wife. The shame of it cut me to the quick." Susannah gripped her chair as if afraid she would fall off. "I tried to make her see sense. I talked myself blue in the face but she refused to listen. She said that he loved her as much as she loved him and when the time was right he was going to leave his wife for her."

One of the oldest lies around, Fargo reflected, and the girl had fallen for it.

"I tried to find out who the man was," Susannah continued. "I asked and pried and snooped in her room but there was never a clue. All she would say was that he was handsome and a gentleman." Susannah snorted in derision. "The vermin seduced my little baby and she called him a gentleman."

"How long had she been seeing him?"

"Tamar wouldn't say," Susannah said. "She clamped up and gave me that look of hers that told me wild horses couldn't drag it out of her. I was worried sick. 'What if you become pregnant?' I asked her. She said the man promised to leave his wife right away if that happened and they would go off together to live happily ever after. Her exact words. Happily ever after. What do you think of that?"

Fargo had learned long ago that people were as stupid as they wanted to be and nothing anyone could say could change them. "It's too bad you couldn't find out who it was."

"I know. I know," Susannah sadly agreed. "You can imagine my predicament. I was the only one who knew her secret. My husband went on with his daily routine, thinking everything was fine, and I didn't dare confide in him. It would have destroyed him to think his pride and joy could stoop so low."

"And then she disappeared," Fargo said.

"Yes." Susannah grimaced with inner hurt. "I thought it couldn't possibly get any worse but it did. She vanished. We searched and searched. Our neighbors helped and townsmen came and Marshal Tibbit organized them, the one thing he's done right. But there was no trace of Tamar anywhere." She looked at Fargo. Tears had formed at the corners of her eyes and were trickling down her cheeks. "I didn't know what to think. Was the married man to blame? Or was it whoever took the first girl, Felicity? And then when those other girls went missing—" She stopped and shook her head. "It's all so confusing."

"It seems to be," Fargo said.

Susannah wiped her face with her sleeve. "Then I heard about you and here I am. Will you accept the money or not?"

"Not," Fargo said, and slid the purse across to her.

"You *do* have scruples."

"I'm not a paid assassin."

"I just hate to think he might get away with it. That Tibbit will arrest him and he'll go on trial and maybe they'll put him in prison instead of being strung up by the neck as he should be."

"I'll do what needs doing," Fargo said. Beyond that, he wasn't willing to make a promise he might not be able to keep.

"If that's how it has to be." Susannah took the purse and slowly rose, a portrait in misery. "I had such high hopes."

Fargo walked around and gently gripped her arms. When she raised her head he looked her in the eyes and said again, "I'll do what needs doing. On that you can count."

"Oh," Susannah said, and then again, more happily, "Oh. I see. In that case you're still welcome to the money."

"No, thanks." Fargo ushered her down the hall. As they came to the parlor Helsa met them and escorted Susannah the rest of the way. Fargo returned to the kitchen, refilled his coffee cup, and sat at the table, pondering.

Helsa came back. She filled her cup and claimed a chair

and stared at him as if expecting him to say something. When he didn't, she said, "Well?"

"Well what?"

"Care to share what the two of you were talking about? I was polite and didn't listen but I would dearly love to know."

"She wouldn't want me to say."

Helsa sipped and set the cup down and folded her fingers around it. "She said an interesting thing as she was leaving."

"About?"

"You."

"Me?"

"Yes. She looked back and said, and I'll quote her, 'He's a good man, that Skye Fargo.' You must have impressed her."

Fargo shrugged.

"Goodness, you talk a body's ears off."

Fargo sat back. A notion had occurred to him, and he said, "I've got a question for you about the first girl, Felicity."

"You won't answer mine but you expect me to answer yours?"

"Is there any chance she might have taken up with a married man before she disappeared?"

It was Helsa's turn to sit back. "So that's what Susannah confided in you." She tapped her cup. "I don't know. Felicity was attractive, and headstrong. It's possible, I suppose." Her brow knit with recollection. "And now that I think of it, my husband was awful secretive about whatever he found out before he disappeared. He mentioned once that he had an idea who was to blame but when I pressed him he wouldn't say anything except that if he was right it was despicable." She looked at Fargo. "My God. You don't think a married man is going around seducing our young girls and then murdering them?"

"Never put anything past anyone," Fargo said.

"Is that your outlook on life? God, how cynical. If I believed like you do, I'd go around all day in the dumps."

"I have the cure up in my room and my invite still holds."

"About having a drink with you? I thought you'd forgotten, what with Susannah's visit."

"Some women say it is all men ever think about," Fargo replied, and grinned.

"After what you said about a married man, I could use a drink. But just one," Helsa cautioned. "And I want you to promise that you'll behave yourself. Your solemn word."

"You have it," Fargo lied.

9

Fargo sat on the bed and Helsa Chatterly sat in the chair. She'd brought two glasses and he had filled them halfway. Now she was studying him over her glass. He pretended not to notice and gazed out the window at a patch of sky sprinkled with stars.

"You puzzle me."

"Works both ways," Fargo said.

"I puzzle you too?" Helsa downed the whiskey without batting an eyelash. "In what regard? I'm a widow who runs a boardinghouse. My life couldn't be any simpler."

"You're a good-looking widow who runs a boardinghouse. And good-looking women usually have a man around."

"My husband was murdered a year ago," Helsa reminded him sharply. "Which you seem to keep forgetting."

"A year ago," Fargo said.

"More than enough time to cope with my grief. Is that what you're suggesting?" Helsa tipped the glass to her lips. "Some of us take longer than others."

"It must be lonely."

Helsa emptied her glass and held out her hand for the bottle. Instead of refilling the glass, she swilled straight from it, several long swallows. She didn't give the bottle back. "Damn you."

"I don't mean to upset you."

"The hell you don't. You want me thinking of him and how him and me used to . . . you know."

"If it bothers you, leave," Fargo said.

"As if you really want me to. I've seen how you look at me. You have one thing on your mind and one thing only."

"I do?"

Helsa raised the bottle again. After a couple of swallows she said, "Conniving devil. You plan to get me drunk so you can have your way with me."

"I'd just as soon you were sober."

"You are full of it up to here." Helsa raised a hand to her chin. "You must think I'm stupid or gullible."

"I think you are as fine a woman as I've ever met," Fargo said in earnest. "Your husband was a lucky man."

"Quit reminding me of him." Helsa got up and moved to the window and drank more whiskey. "I ache when I think of James. Some nights I curl into a ball and cry myself to sleep."

"Maybe you really should go."

Helsa turned and stared at him while taking another swig. "Bastard," she said.

"You are a mean drunk," Fargo said.

"Bastard, bastard, bastard." Helsa came to the bed and stood in front of him. "I could just shoot you."

"For sharing my bottle?"

"For being so damn good-looking." Bending, Helsa pressed her mouth to his. Her lips were warm and wet and soft, and she tasted of whiskey. She kissed lightly at first but with increasing ardor as the kiss went on. When she drew back, her eyes were closed and she was breathing heavily. "That was nice."

"How about a second helping?" Fargo molded his mouth to hers. The kiss lasted longer, and when they broke for breath, Helsa rested her forehead on his chest.

"Oh my."

"Am I still a bastard?"

"More than ever." Yet she kissed him a third time, passionately, fiercely, while her fingers ran lightly over and around his neck and explored his face.

For Fargo's part, he grew as hard as iron. Sliding his hands behind her, he sculpted her shoulders and her shoulder blades, then ran his hands down her back to her bottom. At the contact of his fingers below her waist, she stiffened and exhaled into his mouth.

Presently Helsa pushed on his chest and turned her face to the ceiling. "My head is swimming," she said softly.

"The whiskey," Fargo said.

"No. Not that." A rueful smile spread Helsa's lips. "It's been so long. So very, very long."

Fargo knew the feeling. Whenever he was off on a scout for weeks at a stretch he craved a woman like some men craved tobacco. He kissed her throat and her ear and nipped at the lobe. He licked her neck, kissed her eyebrow, then glued his mouth to hers anew.

Helsa moaned. She removed his hat and dropped it to the floor and entwined her fingers in his hair. Her body gave off heat like the stove.

Cupping her twin mounds, Fargo squeezed them through her dress. They swelled and firmed and he could feel her nipples like tacks against his palms. He pinched them and she squirmed and cooed.

"God, I want you."

For Fargo it was mutual.

"One thing, though," Helsa said, and gripped the front of his shirt. "You're never to tell a soul, you hear? This is between you and me."

"You and me," Fargo repeated.

"I mean it. I pray to God you're not one of those braggarts who boasts of his conquests. No one must ever know."

"If I ever tell anyone," Fargo said, taking her hand, "you can cut this off." He placed her hand on his rigid pole.

Helsa gasped. She glanced down and breathed, "Oh my God! You're so big."

"Like it?" Fargo said, and ran her hand up and down. She didn't draw away. To the contrary, she fondled and stroked him and her breathing became heavier and heavier. She offered no resistance when he eased her onto her back and slid his arm under her legs and lifted them onto the bed. Stretching out beside her, he unbuckled his gun belt and dropped it to the floor.

Helsa kept one hand between his legs and with her other she cupped his chin.

"You're magnificent."

"We're just starting," Fargo said.

She kissed him, hard, and scraped his cheek with a fingernail. "I want to forget, even if it's only for a little while."

Fargo placed a hand on her thigh.

"You have no notion of what it's like," Helsa said. "Wanting someone who isn't there. Wanting *that*, but you can't have it because you're a lady and ladies aren't supposed to have *that* unless they're married. It's not fair how we're treated. Either men put us on pedestals or they treat us like whores."

"Less jabber," Fargo said, and to silence her, he kissed her. At the back of her dress was a row of small buttons that resisted his prying. He had half a mind to rip the dress off but that might spoil her mood so he patiently took his time and at last peeled it down her shoulders to her waist. Underneath she had on a thin cotton chemise and long cotton drawers. No petticoats, much to his delight. He loosened the chemise enough to slide his hand up and under, and cupped her breast.

"Ohhhh," Helsa said.

Fargo massaged and tweaked first one and then the other as their tongues swirled. He sucked on hers and she sucked on his. He lathered her throat and traced the tip of his tongue to her cleavage. The chemise thwarted him. Quickly, he stripped off her dress and her undergarments and tossed them to the floor.

In repose, her face wreathed by her lustrous hair, Helsa Chatterly was breathtaking. Her ample breasts curved to twin peaks, her nipples erect with raw desire. She had a golden thatch to match her golden hair, and winsome legs that seemed to go on forever. Her red lips, puckered in delight, were two cherries waiting to be tasted. "Don't stare at me like that."

"Like what?" Fargo had been momentarily distracted by her beauty.

"It embarrasses me."

"You should be used to it."

"I'm not a saloon tart. You're only the second man in my entire life to see me without any clothes on."

Fargo hadn't realized. He was so accustomed to tarts, as she'd called them, he tended to forget that some women treated their bodies as a rare treasure only a privileged few were allowed to admire.

"I mean it. Stop staring, consarn you, and do something."

"Happy to oblige," Fargo said, and hurriedly shed his boots and pants. Stretching out beside her, he ran his fingertips from her knee to her navel and down the other leg.

Helsa was doing some staring of her own. "You have a lot more muscles than James did. Your stomach in particular." She pressed her palm to his abdomen. "It's like a washboard."

Fargo inhaled her left breast and flicked her nipple. It elicited a loud moan, and she ground her hips against his. Sliding a finger between her legs, he stroked her core; she was wet from wanting him. He went on stroking and she went on grinding until finally he moved between her legs and rose onto his knees. Her eyes hooded with lust, Susannah delicately wrapped her fingers around his member.

"A stallion," she said huskily.

Inserting the tip, Fargo penetrated her. He thrust, and she mewed. He went on thrusting, ever harder and ever faster, and she met each with a push of her hips. She had been so long without it that she was an inferno between her legs. Gripping her buttocks, he rammed more forcefully.

"Yes!" Helsa said, her nails raking his back. "Like that. Do me. Do me hard."

Gradually they rose to the summit. The climax came when

Helsa arched her back and cried out; it sent Fargo hurtling over the brink. Together they coasted on tides of release. Afterward, Fargo lay by her side, drifting in and out. By the clock it was past ten when he rose on an elbow and drank in the vista of her charms. She was asleep, her breasts rising and falling in rhythm to her breathing.

A faint sound downstairs didn't gain Fargo's interest. But a louder sound, the scrape of wood on wood, as of a chair being moved, did. Sitting up, he shook Helsa's hip. She mumbled something and went on sleeping. He shook again and her eyelids cracked in dreamy contentment.

"What?"

"I thought you said your other boarder wasn't coming back tonight."

"He's not." Helsa closed her eyes and went to roll over but stopped when he gripped her shoulder.

"Do you have a dog?"

"No. James and I had one when we were first married but it was run over by a wagon."

"A cat, maybe?"

"Cat fur make me sneeze, so no."

Fargo shook her some more but she pushed his hand away.

"Let me sleep, will you?"

"Listen," Fargo said.

"To what?"

In a few moments the scraping was repeated.

Startled, Helsa sat up and covered her breasts with her arms. "What on earth was that?"

"It's not your dog or your cat."

"You are not at all funny."

"It sounds as if you have another visitor," Fargo suggested.

"Do you honestly think I would come up here with you without bolting both the front and back doors? I couldn't risk

70

someone like the marshal happening by and walking in on us."

From downstairs came a creak.

"My God," Helsa whispered. "Someone *is* down there. That was the door to the pantry. It always makes that noise."

"I'll have a look-see," Fargo offered. He tugged into his buckskin pants and slipped the Colt from its holster and moved toward the door.

"What in heaven's name do you think you're doing?"

"Going downstairs."

"Not like that you're not."

"Not like what?"

"Not half naked. What if it's a friend of mine? Finish getting dressed and then you can go." Helsa slid from the bed and gathered up her dress. "I'll put myself together and be right down."

To Fargo it was foolish. But he pulled on his shirt and slid his feet into his boots and jammed his hat onto his head, and with the Colt in one hand and his gun belt in the other, he cat-footed to the head of the stairs.

From somewhere below came a *scritch-scritch-scritch.*

After the clashes he'd had with the three jackasses, Fargo thought it best to be cautious. He was almost to the bottom when he discerned that the sounds were coming from the kitchen. He rounded the banister and took a step into the hall.

A shadowy shape filled the kitchen doorway.

Fargo caught the glint of metal in the lamplight and flung himself at the floor. Simultaneously, the house rocked to the boom of a large-caliber rifle. A leaden hornet buzzed over his head and struck the front door with a *thwack*. Fargo brought up the Colt but the shadow was gone. Heaving erect, he raced down the hall. The slam of the back door lent wings to his feet. Cocking the Colt, he was across the kitchen and outside almost before the sound died. He darted to the left and crouched to make a small target but no shots rang out.

The backyard was empty. Figuring the shooter had ducked around the side, Fargo flew to the corner and on to the front. The front yard was empty, too. He ran to the gate, pushed it wide, and rushed to the middle of the street.

Other than several townsmen standing in front of the saloon and a rider just leaving town at the far end, the street was deserted.

One of the men in front of the saloon cupped a hand to his mouth. "What's going on over there, mister?"

Another yelled, "What was that shot we just heard?"

Fargo wished to hell he knew.

10

Marshal Tibbit wasn't any too pleased. "Since you hit my town all hell has broken loose. You were nearly lynched. You keeping having fights with Harve and his friends. Now someone sneaks into Helsa's house and takes a shot at you. What is it about you that people want to kill you or hurt you?"

They were in Helsa's parlor. Fargo was in a chair, the lawman on the settee. "You're blaming me?"

"You are a trouble magnet, sir," Tibbit huffed. "And to be frank, I don't like having my sleep disturbed." He had on a coat over a nightshirt and his badge was pinned to the coat. He was hatless and his hair was disheveled.

"Next time I'll ask the shooter to try during the day," Fargo said, and was jolted by a thought. "Then again, maybe he already did."

"How's that?" Tibbit asked.

Fargo told him about the shot in the forest when he was looking for tracks near the canyon.

"Why didn't you inform me of it right away? This is becoming quite serious."

"You're telling me."

Tibbit rubbed his double chins. "Do you know what I think? I think whoever took the girls heard that you are helping me and is trying to eliminate you."

Fargo was thinking the same thing.

"And whoever it is won't stop trying until you're six feet

73

under." Tibbit regarded Fargo with concern. "Perhaps you should move on while you're still breathing."

"You want me to give up?"

"Better that than you end up dead. After all, it's not as if any of this involves you personally. You didn't know any of the missing girls."

Fargo touched his neck where the rope had scraped his skin. "I take it real personal when someone tries to kill me."

"So you're staying?"

"You couldn't make me go."

"Very well." Tibbit stood just as Helsa came into the room carrying a tray with cups of coffee. He smiled and shook his head. "Thank you, my dear, but no, thanks. I have any of that, I won't be able to sleep a lick. And I dearly need my rest." He patted her arm. "I'll see myself out. No need to bother yourself."

Helsa set the tray on a table in front of the settee. "He has no idea about who it was, does he?"

"He doesn't get many ideas, period," Fargo said. She handed him a cup and saucer. The coffee was hot and black, as he liked it. "How many married men are there in Haven?"

"No one has ever counted them. Were I to guess, I'd say well over half. Close to fifty. Probably more."

Fargo frowned. He couldn't very well go around to each and every one.

Word might get to whomever they were after and the killer would light a shuck.

A better way was to have the killer come to him. "Now I know how a worm on a hook feels."

Helsa caught on right away. "You plan to set yourself up as bait."

"Unless you know a better way."

"I wish I did." She came around the table and sat on the settee. "This has been an eventful night in more ways than one," she commented with a warm smile.

"How did he get in?" Fargo wondered.

"I beg your pardon?"

"You told me you made a point of throwing the bolts on the doors so we wouldn't be disturbed. How did the shooter get in?" Fargo rose and went to each of the ground floor windows. All of them were latched.

Helsa had followed, and now she said, "What did he do? Walk in through the walls?"

"That's plain silly," Fargo said. But the hell of it was, how *had* the man gotten inside? He tried to remember if he'd heard the back door bolt being thrown when the shooter ran out, and couldn't. "There's no other way in or out?"

"Not unless he came in through the root cellar."

"Show me."

In a corner of the kitchen on the floor was a small trapdoor. Below were steps and a cellar for keeping vegetables and salted meat and preserves.

Another small door opened onto the backyard. It was partially screened by a lilac bush, which was why Fargo hadn't noticed it before.

"Here's our answer."

"Very few people know about it," Helsa said. "Close friends only."

"Give me a list of names."

"I'll have to think on it some," Helsa said. "Most are women, I'm afraid."

"Women with husbands?"

"Oh. I see what you are getting at."

They went back in. It had been an eventful day and Fargo wearily bent his steps to his room. As he was closing the door Helsa came up and pecked him on the cheek.

"Thank you for earlier."

"Next time bar the root cellar doors, too."

"I'm free tomorrow night." Grinning mischievously, Helsa kissed him on the lips, turned, and sashayed to her bedroom.

"Women," Fargo muttered. He took the precaution of propping a chair against the door and made sure the window was latched. Blowing out the lamp, he lay in bed on his back, the Colt in his right hand.

From now on he had to have eyes in the back of his head. The man he was hunting had turned the tables and was hunting him. And the man had an edge. The man knew who he was; he had no idea who he was after. That edge could prove fatal unless he was God-almighty careful. With that thought Fargo drifted off.

As was his habit he woke at the break of dawn. He washed in the basin and combed his hair and went down to the kitchen. Helsa wasn't up yet so he fired the stove and put a fresh batch of coffee on.

He found eggs and bacon and both were sizzling in pans when Helsa shuffled in wearing a bulky robe, and yawning.

"Goodness, you're an early riser."

Fargo pulled her to him and cupped her bottom and kissed her on the mouth. "In more ways than one."

Helsa pushed him back. "I'm not up two minutes and you want to ravish me again. You are a randy goat, sir." She giggled as she said it. "I much prefer the nighttime, anyway."

Fargo turned to the stove and flipped the bacon over and poked at the scrambled eggs. "Make yourself useful. Have any toast and jam?"

She did, and when they sat down to the table, their plates brimmed with food. Fargo had three slices of toast piled on his. He washed the meal down with five cups of piping hot black coffee. When he was done he sat back and patted his belly.

"If I ate like this every day I'd look like Marshal Tibbit."

"I doubt that," Helsa said. "You're one of those men who likes being hard."

She realized what she had said, and laughed. "Listen to me. I'm becoming as naughty as you."

"Not by a long shot," Fargo said.

"What are your plans for the day?"

"The worm is going to rub this town's nose in its dirt."

"I'm sorry?"

"Later," Fargo said. He got up and went down the street to the general store. The owner had just arrived to open up. Fargo bought a new whetstone and made small talk about the town and the weather and then casually asked, "Did you hear about last night? Someone took a shot at me at the boarding-house."

"My word," the owner declared. "No, I didn't hear. Have you any idea who it was?"

Fargo leaned toward him as if confiding a secret and said quietly, "As a matter of fact, I do. It's the same man who took the missing women."

"Who?" the owner asked excitedly.

Fargo shook his head. "Not yet. By tomorrow night I'll have the proof I need to give the man's name to the marshal. You'll find out when everyone else does." He started to go but stopped to put a finger to his lips. "Can I count on you to keep it quiet?"

"As God is my witness," the owner said.

Fargo walked out into the bright sunlight, and chuckled. The saloon was his next stop. The bartender was sweeping the floor and looked half awake, and mildly surprised.

"I don't open for a couple of hours yet."

"That's too bad," Fargo said. "I could use a drink after the night I had."

"How do you mean?"

Fargo told him about the attempt on his life. He ended by glancing at the batwings and lowering his voice. "Keep it to yourself but I know who it was. By tomorrow night he'll be behind bars."

"You don't say."

Fargo paid visits to the butcher shop, where he asked if the butcher sold jerky and happened to mention his big secret, and then to the livery, where he asked how much it would cost to put up the Ovaro and happened to mention his big secret, and then to the millinery, where he asked how much it would cost to buy a bonnet for a lady friend and happened to mention his big secret.

By midday Fargo had gone from one end of the main street to the other.

He'd confided in every store owner and was feeling immensely pleased with himself.

Given how fast gossip spread in a small town like Haven, he figured every last soul would hear the news by sundown. He passed the marshal's office when suddenly the door opened and out barreled Marion Tibbit.

"Hold it right there. What do you think you're doing?"

"They call it walking," Fargo said.

"I just came from the general store. Becker is telling everyone that you know who took that shot at you."

"Good," Fargo said.

"Why haven't you told me?"

"Because I don't know yet."

"Then why is Becker saying you do?"

"Because I told him I did."

Marshal Tibbit scratched his head. "You're confusing the hell out of me. What purpose does that serve?"

"I want the back-shooter to try again," Fargo said.

Amazement rippled across Tibbit's face. "The devil you say. Are you trying to get yourself killed?"

"Not if I can help it." Fargo walked on to Chatterly's. He opened the gate and went to the steps and up them to the front door. He didn't bother to knock but walked on in and made for the kitchen. He was almost to the parlor when Harvey Stansfield stepped out in front of him. Harvey was holding a new ax handle. In the parlor stood McNee and Dugan with ax handles of their own.

"Hell," Fargo said.

"We have you now, you son of a bitch," Harvey declared.

"Were you born stupid or do you work at it?"

Harvey roared like a shot bear and raised the handle like

78

a club. A near-maniacal expression came over him and he swung at Fargo's head. Fargo ducked, slammed a fist into Harvey's gut, and spun to meet the charges of McNee and Dugan. They were so eager to get at him that they bumped shoulders and Dugan shoved McNee so he would be first. Fargo punched Dugan in the mouth and Dugan fell back against McNee. Harvey was straightening and hissing and he thrust the end of the handle at Fargo's stomach. Pivoting, Fargo felt it brush his buckskins.

He brought both fists up, boxing Harvey's ears, and Harvey howled and skipped away. Dugan had recovered and was coming at him again and Fargo got his hands up as the ax handle swept down. He grabbed it, wincing at the pain in his palms, and wrenched it from Dugan's grasp. Before Dugan could recover his wits, Fargo drove the handle into Dugan's gut, folding him like wet paper. Not slowing for an instant, Fargo arced the handle up and around and was rewarded with the *thunk* of it connecting with Dugan's head. Dugan collapsed, and over him vaulted McNee, whooping fiercely. Wood clacked on wood as Fargo blocked several blows and then swung at McNee's face. McNee deflected it, feinted right but went left, and caught Fargo on the shoulder. Pain and numbness shot down Fargo's arm. He almost lost his grip. McNee hiked his ax handle, and Fargo kicked him in the knee.

Yowling in agony, McNee retreated into the parlor and Fargo went after him, swinging. McNee raised his ax handle to protect his head and Fargo slashed down and in across McNee's legs. McNee started to buckle but stayed on his feet. A parry, a sidestep, and Fargo smashed the handle against McNee's ear.

That left Harvey.

Fargo whirled just as Stansfield came at him. Their ax handles became blurs. The whack of wood on wood was near continuous. The brute force of Harvey's rage drove Fargo back, but only a few steps. Fargo absorbed a blow to the ribs, countered with one of his own, and when Harvey clutched at his side, smashed him across the fingers. Harvey swore and turned to run and Fargo hit him across the back of the head.

Helsa was on the stairs, staring in shock.

"I could use some coffee," Fargo said.

"You beat all three of them."

"They are good practice for swatting flies."

"I never saw anyone move as fast as you."

Fargo leaned the handle against the wall. "I'll go fetch the marshal if you'll put that coffee on."

In a rush and a rustle of her dress Helsa had his hand in both of hers. "Are you hurt?"

"A few more bruises," Fargo said.

"I saw most of it. I'll gladly testify in a court of law if you press charges," she offered.

"I just want them out of my hair for a while," Fargo enlightened her.

Helsa stared at their still forms and then at him, and grinned. "There's never a dull moment with you around, is there?"

11

The ponderosa pines were alive with movement and sounds. Robins warbled and jays screeched. Chipmunks scampered zanily about. From a high limb a tuft-eared squirrel chewed on a pinecone and watched Fargo ride underneath the tree it was in.

Fargo rode with the Henry across his saddle. He had learned his lesson the day before. He was ready to answer lead with lead, even if the shots fired at him came from some distance.

It was autumn but the heat of summer had not given way to the chill that would herald winter and the sun hung yellow and hot in the afternoon sky. Fargo was alone. He had snuck out of Haven without—he hoped—anyone spotting him. He didn't want Tibbit along. The lawman meant well but he was a bundle of awkwardness waiting for an accident to happen.

Wild, remote, haunt of the Apache and home to the Navaho, Arizona Territory had yet to be fully explored. A white man took his life in his hands every time he ventured beyond the safe limits of a town. As if that were not enough to keep Fargo on edge, a madman was out to kill him. A man who snatched young women from their backyards—and did what to them? That was the question that burned in Fargo like a bonfire. He could guess, but the truth might be worse.

The pines thinned at the brink of the canyon. Fargo drew rein and dismounted. He let the reins dangle and moved to the spot where he had lost the trail. Below was the undisturbed talus, and below that, a slope dotted with boulders. He couldn't see what was below them.

Fargo sat down and eased over the side. He slid several feet on the loose stones and dirt, raising curlicues of dust. When he stopped sliding he propped the Henry's stock on the talus and used it to lever to his feet. The talus didn't shift as he expected. He took a tentative step and nothing happened. Another step, and another, then the rattle of a small stone—the talus held. He poked at it, seeking to assess how deep the loose dirt and rocks were.

"I'll be damned."

The stock sank only an inch. Kneeling, Fargo set the Henry down and dug at the talus with his fingers.

"What the hell?"

Never in all his wide travels had Fargo come across a talus slope with so little talus. It was almost as if—he raised his head and scanned the side of the canyon for as far as he could see. This was the only talus patch. Relying on the Henry as a crutch, he stood and edged lower until he was on firm footing. A pair of enormous boulders blocked his view. He moved between them and nearly stepped in a line of pockmarks: horse tracks.

Son of a bitch, Fargo thought. The man the townsfolk called the Ghoul had spread the rocks and dirt himself to make everyone think it was talus.

The Ghoul would ride down it, dismount, then go back on foot and smooth the loose dirt and rocks over so that from above it appeared that a horse hadn't crossed.

Fargo turned and climbed to the rim. He shoved the Henry into the scabbard to free both hands for riding and climbed on the Ovaro. He gigged the stallion over the rim and down onto the stones and dirt. For one of the few times ever, the Ovaro balked. Fargo tapped his spurs and the stallion took a few steps and stopped. "It's all right, boy," he said, and patted its neck. Another tap of his spurs and the Ovaro moved slowly down, stones clattering from under its hooves.

Once past the fake talus the footing was better but Fargo still had to exercise care. The trail was well marked, showing that his quarry had come and gone many times by the same devious route.

Over half an hour of cautious riding brought Fargo to the bottom. Drawing rein, he scanned the canyon. A quarter of a mile across at its widest, it was bordered on the north by ocher sandstone cliffs that reared hundreds of feet high. Bends in both directions prevented him from seeing how long it was. He reined to the west. High walls towered and the canyon narrowed until it was barely wide enough for a wagon.

Suddenly Fargo heard what he took to be the clank and rattle of pots and pans. Puzzled, he put his hand on his Colt. The next moment he rounded a bend and came face-to-face with a man, who was as surprised to see him as he was to discover the source of the clanking.

It was a prospector: a bewhiskered, wizened gent in worn clothes and a hat with holes in it, leading a burro heaped with tools and grub. He was carrying an old Sharps rifle with tacks in the stock, an Indian trademark. "Where the blazes did you come from?" he blurted, and started to raise the Sharps.

A flick of Fargo's hand and the Colt was out and the hammer thumbed back. "I wouldn't," he said.

The prospector blinked. "Hold on, there, sonny. I wouldn't really shoot you."

"I'd shoot you," Fargo said. "Set that buffalo gun of yours down and do it as slow as molasses."

"And get dirt on it?"

Fargo thought that hilarious, given the man was caked with dust from his tattered hat to his scuffed boots.

"Can't I just lean it against my leg?"

"Flat at your feet."

"You're a mean one," the prospector complained but he did as Fargo wanted. "There. I hope you're happy. You can put away that hogleg now."

Fargo kept it trained on him. "Who are you?"

"Folks call me Badger, on account I'm always digging in the ground. Been roaming this highland for going on ten years now." Badger smiled, showing more gaps than teeth. "Ask anyone and they'll tell you I'm as friendly as can be."

"How did you get down here?"

Badger pumped his arms up and down and did a good imitation of a crow.

"Caw! Caw!" Cackling, he said, "I flapped my wings and flew."

"I'd really like to know."

Pointing back the way he came, Badger said, "I walked here. How else? You ask damn fool questions."

"Seen anyone?"

"Besides you?" Badger shook his head. "Not in a coon's age. I fight shy of people. Haven't set foot in a town in nigh on half a year and wouldn't know where any was."

Fargo bobbed his head to the south. "There's one called Haven half a day's walk."

Badger's eyes crinkled at the rim. "So that's where."

"Where what?"

"I figured one must be close." Badger scratched under an arm and sniffed his fingers. "Where are you bound, anyhow?"

"I'm hunting a man who had a young woman with him. Maybe you've seen them?"

"I just told you I fight shy of folks," Badger said. "What do they look like?"

"I don't know."

"You're hunting for them and you don't know who you're hunting? Mister, folks say I'm touched in the head but you have me beat." Badger stooped to pick up his Sharps. "If you don't mind I'll be on my way."

Fargo reined aside. The ore hound smiled and tugged on the lead rope. The burro was almost past the Ovaro when splash of color caused Fargo to rein in close to it. "Hold it," he commanded.

"What now?" Badger said.

Fargo bent and snatched the object that had caught his attention: a blue bonnet, hanging by its straps from a pick handle. "Where did you get this?"

"I don't remember," Badger said. "I've had it quite a spell."

Fargo didn't believe him. The fabric was new. The bonnet hadn't been worn more than a few times. And he recalled someone saying that Myrtle Spencer had been wearing a blue dress when she disappeared. He sniffed it and caught the lingering scent of perfume. "I want the truth."

"Who do you think you are?" Badger bristled. A wild gleam came into his eyes and he lunged and grabbed the bonnet from Fargo's hand and held it close to his chest. "This is mine, you hear me! Mine, mine, mine!"

"Where did you get it?" Fargo asked again.

"I don't remember." Badger unbuttoned two of the buttons on his shirt and stuffed the bonnet under it.

"Yes, you do."

Badger picked up the lead rope to the burrow and glared. "I don't think I like you. I don't think I like you even a little bit."

Fargo exercised patience. "The woman who wore that has gone missing. I'm looking for her."

"She's one of those you don't know how they look?" Badger shook his head. "If you don't know, how would I?"

"It's important," Fargo persisted. "The man who took her might have killed her."

Badger gazed back the way he had come and a shudder shook him. "The skin man," he said.

"The what?"

"The skin man. He likes to run his hands over it."

"Who does?"

Badger glanced around and crooked a finger at Fargo and said in a whisper, "I've seen what he does. I'm sneaky when I need to be and I snuck right up and I saw."

"Saw what?"

"What I shouldn't have. It's why I stay away from towns. I've always known. From when I was young, and my uncle."

"You're not making any damn sense."

"I am to me," Badger said, and tittered. "You would savvy if you were me but you're not so you don't. Stay away from them, mister. They're rotten apples, all of them. Oh, they look all shiny on the outside but they're rotten as sin on the inside."

"Who is?"

"What have we been talking about? People." Badger tugged on the rope and started down the canyon, the burro plodding doggedly behind.

Fargo reined the Ovaro next to him. "I mean it. I need to know about that bonnet."

"What bonnet?"

"The one you stuck in your shirt."

Badger put his hand on the bulge and his mouth split in his mostly toothless grin. "I never had me a bonnet before. I could have taken the dress but he'd be bound to notice it was missing, it being so new and all."

"Who would? The skin man?"

"The beast."

"Why do you call him that?"

Badger stopped and looked up. "We're all beasts but he's one of the worst. He ever finds out I know, there's no telling what he'll do."

"The people in Haven call him the Ghoul."

"Do they, now? Well, it fits." Badger motioned as if shooing him away. "Now leave me be. Maybe I'll visit that town you mentioned. I am low on tobacco and I can't do without." He tugged and hiked away, muttering under his breath.

Fargo almost climbed down to stop him. But it might do little good; the ore hound's mind wandered all over the place. A better idea was to backtrack and see where Badger came from. He could always catch up later and press the old goat for answers.

Fargo reined around. The burro's tracks paralleled the horse prints he had been following. Presently the canyon floor widened and the sandstone gave way to forested slopes. Another quarter of a mile, and the tracks diverged. Fargo came to a stop. The horse prints bore to the northeast; the burro's tracks to the northwest. How could that be, he asked himself, if the old prospector had been spying on the Ghoul? He reined to the northeast, through dense woodland that was strangely silent. He didn't hear birds or squirrels. Not even the buzz of a locust.

Reaching down, Fargo shucked the Henry. Animals never went quiet without cause. A prowling meat-eater would do it, or it could be something—or someone—else.

The trail led into tall pines. Needles carpeted the ground inches thick and the prints were harder to make out. Fargo came to a small clearing.

The prints ended in the middle. Past that spot, the needles were unbroken. He drew rein and climbed down. It seemed impossible. A horse couldn't vanish into thin air. But it could *seem* to if the man had used the Comanche trick of wrapping its hooves in swaths of fur.

"No doubt about it," Fargo said out loud. "You're clever as hell."

A horse was heavy enough that even with fur over its hooves it left impressions in dust and soft soil. But on a thick layer of pine needles it left precious few and the needles would smooth out after a little while just as if the horse never stepped on them.

Fargo refused to give up. Faint signs went off to the north and so did he, walking and leading the Ovaro. It was slow going. Several times he lost the trail and had to rove about to find it again.

The pines gave way to ground made up of near solid rock.

Fargo swore. Beyond the rock reared a series of cliffs that no horse could climb. He gazed at the high rims and caught the gleam of sunlight on metal. Instantly, he spun and vaulted into the saddle. Lead spanged off the rock where he had been standing even as the thunder of the shot crashed and echoed. Fargo raced for the woods. Another boom, and a slug whizzed past the stallion's head. He reined right and then left, zigzagging to make the Ovaro harder to hit. Then he was under cover and drawing rein. Leaping down, he darted to the edge of the trees and hunkered behind a bole. The gleam high up was gone. He waited, hoping the shooter would show himself, but no such luck.

"Damn."

By now the sun was low in the western sky. Fargo had a choice. Stay there all night and seek a way up or around in the morning, or go back to Haven and return at dawn after a good night's sleep—or a night of making love to his landlady.

It really wasn't any choice at all.

12

Night had fallen by the time Fargo reached Haven. He was surprised to find clusters of people the length of the main street talking in hushed tones.

When he rode past they fell silent and stared. He wondered if another woman had gone missing.

The boardinghouse was quiet. A lamp glowed in the parlor. Helsa was on the settee, knitting, and on seeing him she rose and came over and put her hand on his chest.

"Finally, you're back. Where have you been?"

"I was playing cat and mouse with the Ghoul," Fargo informed her. "Any chance of getting something to eat after I wash up?"

"The Ghoul?" Helsa said. "How can that be when Marshal Tibbit has him behind bars?"

Fargo didn't wait for an explanation. He turned and hurried out. More than a dozen townsmen were gathered in front of the jail and he had to shoulder through them. He overheard a few comments.

". . . wait for the circuit judge . . ."

". . . we should try him ourselves . . ."

"Try him, hell. He's guilty as sin. We should take the son of a bitch out and string him up."

The door was barred on the inside. Fargo knocked, and when no one came, he knocked louder.

"Who is it?" Marshal Tibbit asked.

Fargo told him. The bar grated and the door was flung wide and Tibbit pulled him inside and slammed the door shut.

"Thank God. I can use some help." Tibbit replaced the bar and went to his desk and wearily sank into his chair. "You saw them out there?"

Fargo nodded.

"A while ago they demanded I turn him over to them but I refused." Tibbit removed his hat and ran his sleeve across his perspiring brow. "They want to lynch him but I'll be damned if they will."

"Him?" Fargo said. The cell was shrouded in shadow and the figure on the cot in the corner had his back to them.

"I caught the killer," Marshal Tibbit said proudly. "He rode into town and made the biggest mistake he could." Tibbit opened a drawer and took out a blue bonnet and placed it on his desk. "The fool waved this around at the saloon for all to see. It belongs to Myrtle Spencer."

Fargo went to the bars. "Hello, Badger."

The prospector rolled over and bared his toothless grin. "Well, look who it is. Did you find the skin man?"

"He took shots at me."

"And you're still breathing? He's a good shot. I saw him drop a buck once at pretty near two hundred yards."

Tibbit came over. "You know this man?"

"We've met," Fargo said.

"He won't tell me his real name. Claims he took the bonnet from a pile of clothes but he won't say where the pile was or anything about Myrtle."

"He's not the Ghoul," Fargo said.

"I have my doubts," Tibbit said. "But he had the bonnet and he wouldn't or couldn't explain how he got it so I had to arrest him. Word has spread. You saw them out there. They've pretty much made up their minds and want to hang him."

"Your good citizens sure are fond of rope."

"Can you blame them? Five of their own, missing. Four of them women, no less." Tibbit nodded at the prospector. "Maybe he's not the Ghoul but he's a handy scapegoat."

Badger got up and stepped to the bars. "I didn't do anything but take that bonnet. They can't hang a man for that."

"I'll protect you," Tibbit said.

Just then there was loud pounding on the door and voices were raised in anger.

"Open up, Marshal!"

"We want him!"

"We're not leaving until you hand him over!"

Tibbit hitched at his pants and put his hand on his revolver. "Go away!" he yelled. "Disperse to your homes and leave this to the law."

"We'll break the door down if we have to!" a man warned. "Or get some powder and blow it open!"

"Did you hear that?" Tibbit asked in amazement. "People I have known for years." He gnawed on his lip. "I've never faced a mob before. What would you suggest I do?"

Fargo stepped to the gun cabinet. He opened it and took down an English-made shotgun. A drawer under the cabinet contained shells. He loaded both barrels and went to the front door. "When I say, open it quick."

"You're not fixing to blow them to kingdom come, are you?"

"That depends on them."

"Moments like these, I wish I was back selling ladies' corsets." Tibbit removed the bar.

"Now," Fargo said.

The lawman gulped.

The crowd had swollen to twenty or better and were pressed close under the overhang. When the door swung open those nearest to it turned. "What the hell?" a man blurted.

Fargo recognized the voice of the one who had threatened to use powder. He jammed the twin muzzles against the

91

man's cheek and thumbed back the hammers. "Twitch and I splatter your brains."

Everyone froze. Eyes widened in alarm and anger, and a man in a bowler started to slip a hand under his jacket.

"Anyone pulls on me and I cut loose," Fargo warned.

The man in the bowler lowered his hand.

"Oh God," said the one the muzzles were gouging. "Be careful with that cannon, mister. It goes off and it's liable to blow my head clean off."

"Back into the street, all of you," Fargo told them. "I have a few words to say."

All eyes on the shotgun, they retreated and were joined by others who had witnessed the turn of events. No one spoke. Some coughed and fidgeted.

Marshal Tibbit came out and stood on Fargo's right, his six-shooter level. "I should arrest every one of you."

From the back of the crowd came an angry shout, "All we want is for the killer to swing!"

Fargo raised his own voice. "Can all of you hear me?" he asked, and when several at the back nodded, he went on. "It's only right you want to see justice done. But that prospector in there isn't the Ghoul."

"How do you know?" a woman demanded.

"Because while you were working yourselves up to hang an innocent man, the real Ghoul was taking shots at me."

A townsman said, "Why should we believe you? You're not one of us. You're a stranger."

"I want the son of a bitch as much as you do. He's tried three times now to kill me."

"You're sure about that old buzzard in there?"

"If he was the Ghoul I'd shoot him myself."

Murmuring broke out. A few heated exchanges erupted. Fargo let them get it out of their system. When they began to quiet, he raised his arm to get their attention. "Do as the marshal says and go home."

Tibbit stepped off the boardwalk. "You heard the scout.

I want this street cleared." He moved among them, goading them to move along.

Fargo went back into the office. He broke the shotgun open, extracted the shells, and dropped them in the drawer. As he was placing the shotgun on the rack, Badger pressed his face between the cell bars.

"Am I going to be lynched?"

"Not today."

"You did me a favor, buckskin. I'm obliged, and I'd like to do you a favor in return." Badger glanced at the front door. "Come here," he whispered. "I have a secret to tell you."

Fargo went over.

"You wanted to know where I got that bonnet. I can tell you right where to find the pit."

"Did you say pit?" Fargo said.

"The bonnet and the leg," Badger said. "I only kept the leg a little while because it stunk so bad."

"Did you say *leg*?"

Badger motioned for him to come closer. "No one else can hear but you and you have to promise not to say."

Fargo bent his ear to the bars. "I'm listening."

"That's good," Badger said.

There was a tug on Fargo's holster and he glanced down to find it empty.

He went to straighten, only to have his own Colt jammed against his ribs.

"Stand real still or you're a goner." Badger thumbed back the hammer.

"Hell," Fargo said.

Badger cackled. "I sure suckered you, didn't I? As if I'd tell you where the pit was. You'd make him stop and spoil everything. I wouldn't get anymore treats."

Fargo debated trying to pull away but he was bound to be shot. "What the hell are you talking about?"

"The skin man doesn't know I know or that I take things. He wouldn't let me if he did."

"Does this skin man have a name?"

"I never asked."

Boots clomped, and Marshal Tibbit came in and closed the door behind him.

Without looking over at them he said, "I thank you for your help. I couldn't have dispersed them without you."

"Ain't he polite?" Badger said.

Tibbit walked to the desk and was about to slump into his chair when he glanced at the cell. "What on earth?"

"It's like this," Badger said. "Unlock this door or buckskin, here, meets his Maker."

Tibbit started to lower his hand to his revolver but stopped. "How could you let this happen?" he asked Fargo.

"It's not his fault," Badger said, and cackled. "I'm tricky when I need to be. Now get off your fat ass and do as I told you."

"I am not fat," Tibbit said angrily. "I am mildly plump."

"Then get your mildly plump ass over here." Badger did more cackling and gouged Fargo harder. "He's got a puny thinker, the marshal does."

Rising with his arms out from his sides, Tibbit approached the cell. "What do you intend to do with us?"

"Turn about is fair, they say. Open this door."

The key hung from a peg. Tibbit took it down and inserted it in the lock and twisted. At the click, he hesitated. "I have an offer for you."

Badger was as puzzled as Fargo. "What kind of offer?"

"I keep forty dollars and eighteen cents in a cigar box in the bottom drawer on the right. It's yours if you'll spare us."

"You're paying me not to kill you?" Badger snickered. "Why didn't I think of that?" He stepped back and pointed the Colt at the marshal. "Open the door and turn around."

"Please," Tibbit said. "My true calling is corsets."

"This town should pick law with backbone," Badger said. He trained the Colt on Fargo and slowly sidled out, staying well clear of them so they couldn't grab him. "In you go."

"Hell," Fargo said again.

"You don't do it," Badger said, "and I'll shoot lunkhead, here, in his mildly plump ass."

"No one ever tried to shoot me when I sold corsets," Tibbit said.

Fargo sighed and went in and over to the bunk. He sat with his back to the wall and lowered his hand to his boot.

"Your turn," Badger told Tibbit. The marshal nodded and glumly began to back into the cell.

"Hold it." Badger relieved him of his revolver and the key on the ring, gave Tibbit a push, and slammed the door. "How about this?" he said with a grin. "You say your true calling is corsets? I thought mine was gold but maybe I should be an outlaw. I am damn good at this jail breaking business."

"I need a drink," Fargo said.

"Someone will come along soon enough, I reckon," Badger said. He put the key and the Colt on the desk but stuck the marshal's Remington under his belt.

"Where's Gladys?" he asked.

Tibbit gripped the bars and leaned his forehead against them. "Who?"

"Gladys, my burro. What did you do with her? You'd better not have ate her. I eat my own when they get too old."

"How do they taste?" Tibbit asked.

Fargo looked at them and shook his head. He raised his hand to his lap and stretched out on his back and put his arm over his eyes.

"They taste sort of like horses only different," Badger was saying. "You want to boil the meat to soften it some."

"Yours is at the stable," Tibbit said. "So are your packs and tools. I put her up at the town's expense."

"That was kind of you. I take back what I said about your plump ass."

Badger went to the gun rack and took down his Sharps, then moved to the front door. He peeked out, and cackled. "Awful kind, too, to clear the street like you done." He opened the door all the way. "What happened to my bonnet, by the way?"

"I gave it to the mother of the girl it belonged to," Tibbit said.

"That's a shame. I like to wear it at night when I turn in." Badger waved and closed the door and was gone.

"That went well," Marshal Tibbit said.

Skye Fargo swore.

13

They spent the night in the cell. Shortly after seven a.m. Tibbit looked out the window and spied a wagon coming down the street and yelled loud enough to shake the walls. A farmer coming in to deliver eggs to the general store heard him, pulled up, and came in.

"Why, Marshal, what on earth are you doing locked in your own cell?"

"It's a long story, Phillip. Just get us out. The keys are on the desk."

Fargo didn't waste a minute. He went straight to the boardinghouse. Helsa Chatterly was up and in the kitchen fixing breakfast.

"Look at what the cat drug in," she said in a tone that told him she was miffed. "I kept expecting you to show and when you didn't I figured you had gone to the saloon and found someone else to spend the night with."

"I spent it with Tibbit," Fargo said.

"I beg your pardon?"

Fargo told her, and while she chuckled he went up and washed and retied his bandanna. When he came down the food was on the table. The aroma made his stomach growl. He ate six flapjacks with maple syrup and washed them down with four cups of scalding black coffee. He also had a slice of cantaloupe that he salted until it tasted more of salt than cantaloupe.

Helsa watched him eat. "You sure were famished," she stated the obvious as he pushed his plate away.

Fargo was also mad as hell at being outwitted by an old prospector who barely had half a wit to boast of, and having to spend the night listening to Tibbit whine and pace and go on and on about ladies' corsets. He didn't tell her that.

"I'll be gone most of the day."

"You're off after the Ghoul again?"

"And the old prospector," Fargo said.

"What do you make of him? It was a shock, him showing up with Myrtle's bonnet."

"He knows who took the women and where the man is lying low," Fargo said, "and he's going to tell me."

"You won't hurt him, will you? He didn't harm you or Marshal Tibbit."

"That will be up to him." Fargo rose and walked around the table and she stood in his way and placed her hands on his shoulders.

"Be careful out in those wilds. It's not just the Ghoul you have to watch out for."

Fargo knew that better than anyone.

"If you make it back tonight I'll treat you to a special meal. Don't worry about the time." Helsa paused. "I'm sorry I didn't come looking for you last night. I assumed, and I shouldn't have."

"You're the only woman in this town I care to bed."

"Thank you for the compliment," Helsa said. "At least, I think it was one. Or maybe I need to reexamine my morals."

"Oh, hell." Fargo kissed her and left. He went out the front door. The Ovaro was at the hitch rail. He was halfway to the gate when the drum of boots warned him. He whirled, and they were on him—Harvey and Dugan and McNee. Their faces were bruised and swollen and grim with purpose. They hadn't brought the ax handles this time; they came at him with their fists, all three of them in a rush. He barely got his arms up and they were on him, slamming into him and bearing him to the ground.

Fargo smiled grimly. When he was mad he liked to hit things, and he had plenty to hit. He punched Harvey in the face as he went down and smashed a fist into McNee's cheek and planted his boot in Dugan's gut. He absorbed blows without hardly feeling them. He kicked McNee in the leg and McNee yelped and staggered. That left Harvey to try and hold him down alone and Harvey wasn't strong enough. With a heave Fargo gained his feet, raised his fists, and waded in.

"Get him!" Harvey hollered.

Dugan tried. Fargo blocked a left and countered with an uppercut. McNee had regained his balance and walked into a cross that sent him staggering again. Harvey hissed like a snake and flailed his fists in a windmill of rage. Fargo punched him in the mouth, pivoted, and drove his fist into Harvey's wind cage. Dugan clipped him on the chin but not hard enough to jolt him and Fargo returned the favor with a lightning jab. He traded blows with the other two and then Dugan leaped back again and it was all three of them. Fargo reveled in the violence.

He was a whirling dervish, unleashing a storm of straight arms, crosses, uppercuts and jabs. In their eagerness to pound him into the ground, Dugan and McNee collided. It caused both to stumble, and Fargo had his opening. He rammed a right from the shoulder with all his weight behind it and Dugan went down face first. McNee frantically tried to ward off jabs and never saw the left that looped down and in and nearly drove his gut through his backbone.

That left Harvey. Bloodied and panting, he glared and spat, "You son of a bitch. We'll keep doing this until we beat you."

"Good," Fargo said. He feinted right and went right and Harvey teetered on his heels, his eyelids fluttering. A solid cross hurt Fargo's knuckles. It also brought Harvey crashing down.

Fargo's chest was heaving. He looked up, and Helsa was on the porch, her eyes wide.

"Do you want me to fetch the marshal?"

"No."

"But they keep attacking you. They should be behind bars."

"They'd only come after me as soon as they got out."

"The next time they might pull their guns on you. Did you ever think of that?"

"Yes," Fargo said.

"I'm going to get Tibbit anyway. If you won't press charges I'll at least have them thrown off my property and warned never to set foot on it again."

"You do what you have to."

Fargo collected the Ovaro and was on his way out of Haven two hours later than he would have been if Badger hadn't locked them in the cell.

The morning was bright and blue. Songbirds sang and deer bounded off with their tails up. A red hawk sought prey.

Fargo made a beeline for the canyon and rode along the canyon floor to the north and on into the dense timber. When he came in sight of the cliffs he slowed.

Where the trees ended he drew rein, climbed down, and spent the next half an hour studying the cliffs. He didn't show himself. The killer might be up there with his rifle. But nothing moved. There were no glints of metal.

Fargo rubbed his sore jaw where Dugan had clipped him and settled down for a long wait. Another quarter of an hour went by, and the clatter of pots and pans brought him to his feet.

Badger was leading Gladys along the base of the cliffs. He was smiling and singing and happy as a bluebird.

Fargo stayed hidden. He saw Badger hike to a point where two cliffs merge and turn to a solid wall of rock. Prospector and burro walked into the rock and out of sight.

"How the hell?" Fargo said. He let a few minutes go by and climbed on the Ovaro. A flick of the reins and he was out of the trees. His skin crawled with the expectation of taking a slug but not a single shot thundered from on high. He trotted to the spot where Badger and Gladys had vanished, and drew rein.

The cliff didn't merge. There was a narrow gap, wide enough for a rider, leading to who-knew-where. Faint impressions in the dirt hinted that Gladys wasn't the only animal to go through. Unless Fargo was mistaken, those impressions had been made by horse hooves wrapped in fur.

"Got you," Fargo said, and grinned. He gigged the Ovaro and ramparts of rock rose on either side, blotting out most of the sunlight. The gap seemed to go on forever. He thought at any moment it would end, but it didn't. By his reckoning he had gone more than half a mile when the cliffs gave way to a broad expanse of caprock and hard ground. In the far distance a black mesa reared.

Fargo drew rein. He rose in the stirrups but couldn't spot Badger and Gladys anywhere. The burro's prints were easy enough to follow—for a few dozen yards. Then the caprock began, and tracking became a tedious exercise of looking for scrapes and chinks, however slight. At first Fargo thought the trail was leading toward the black mesa but it led to the south of it, across miles of hot wasteland. The sun burned like a furnace. A lizard skittered from his path. He glimpsed the tail end of a snake slithering under a large flat rock; the tail had rattles.

The ground was nearly solid rock. Fargo found it increasingly harder to find sign. The minutes crawled into an hour and another hour. He was sweaty and thirsty and would like to rest but there was no cover, only the burning sun and the hot rock and the lizards and snakes.

When next Fargo glanced toward the black mesa he was to the west of it, and a lot closer. Almost as if Badger were taking a roundabout route to get there. Maybe it was the same route the Ghoul took, Fargo reflected. The better to hide his trail. This near, he saw that the mesa was sprinkled with dark pines and split by shadowed arroyos and recesses. Just the sort of place Apaches might use as a sanctuary—or a white man who kidnapped white women.

A flapping sound made Fargo forget the mesa. Turkey vultures were rising into the air directly ahead, their bald heads a vivid red. Their great wings rising and falling, they slowly gained altitude, moving faster as they climbed in ever widening spirals. He had the illusion they were coming out of the ground, but that couldn't be.

Then the stink washed over him in an invisible wave of loathsome odor.

Fargo almost gagged. Quickly, he adjusted his bandanna so it was over his nose and mouth, sparing him from the worst of the reek. The Ovaro didn't like it, either, and whinnied and shied. Fargo gigged it on to a basin about twenty yards across. A few straggling carrion eaters sluggishly sought the sky, one passing so close, he could count every feather.

Fargo had come across gruesome sights in his travels: pilgrims in a Conestoga, butchered by the Sioux; Mexican freighters, tortured by Apaches; a backwoodsman, clawed to death by a bear. But *this* was more gruesome than any of those. This was something different, something unnatural, something vile.

The basin had become a charnel pit. Bodies and pieces of bodies covered the bottom. Some of the remains were animal: deer skulls and hide and legs, the bones of bears, the complete skeleton of a horse, and a host of smaller bones from the likes of rabbits and raccoons. Most, but not all, had been stripped of flesh.

It was the other remains that interested Fargo: the human remains. Only four women had gone missing so it stood to reason there would be four bodies, or parts from four. But there were more, and not all of them were female.

Fargo counted nine human skulls. None of the skeletons was intact from the neck down. Judging by how the bones were scattered, it appeared to him that they had been chopped into chunks and pieces. He remembered Badger saying something about finding a leg, and put two and two together.

A splash of color on the other side prompted Fargo to circle around and dismount. Scarcely breathing for the stench, he descended. At the bottom was a pile of clothes with other garments scattered about—dresses and shirts and pants and boots and shoes. His nose and throat felt raw and when he took a breath his stomach tried to crawl up his throat. Flies rose in swarms. Maggots infested the rotting flesh. Fargo had to force himself to squat and examine the clothing. All the dresses were torn as if they had been ripped from the women who wore them.

All had a musty smell, as of long neglect, and were covered with dust.

Tufts of human hair poked from under the putrid mass of a dead doe. Fargo gripped the deer's leg and flipped the carcass over. His insides did another flip-flop.

The hair was attached to a human head severed at the neck. A woman's head, the skin long gone and the eyes long since rotted out or pecked out by the buzzards.

One of the first girls taken, Fargo figured. He lifted some of the clothes but couldn't find any clue to who owned them. A crumpled dress lay to one side. He lifted it and shook it and a large black scorpion fell out and landed near his foot. Pincers waving, it raised its tail. Fargo jumped back. He went to put his hand down for balance and nearly put it on another scorpion.

The stink, the maggots, the flies—Fargo had to get out of there. He turned and scrambled up the side and reached for the Ovaro's reins—only someone else had hold of them. "You," he said.

"Me," Badger answered, and cackled.

"You're becoming a thorn in my side."

"I like to think of myself as a pretty rose." Badger was pointing his Sharps and the hammer was cocked. Marshal Tibbit's Remington was tucked under his belt.

Fargo looked but didn't see the burro. "Where did you come from?" He regretted it each time he opened his mouth; the reek was worse.

"Now you see me, now you don't."

"How can you breathe?" Fargo marveled.

"Easy." Badger sucked a breath deep into his lungs and exhaled, smiling the while. "I've been doing it since I was in diapers. Comes natural by now."

"You are a card."

"Thought I was a thorn?"

Fargo nodded at the Sharps. "Don't point that at me."

"Don't tell me what to do," Badger rejoined, and held out the Ovaro's reins. "You take these and I'll take your six-gun."

"You don't want to do this."

"Sure I do. This makes twice I've got the better of you."

"It's no game," Fargo said.

"Never thought it was." The prospector backed off and gestured with the Sharps toward the mesa. "Walk that way. You'll know when to stop."

"Lower that rifle and we'll forget this ever happened."

"Listen to you. I'm the one can blow you to hell if you so much as move wrong." Badger's voice hardened. "Do as I told you and walk."

A dozen yards, and Fargo came on a another, smaller, basin. It was empty except for Gladys, who stood at the bottom dozing. "So this was where."

"I knew someone was following me. Caught sight of you when you came out of the cliffs." Badger made a *tsk-tsk* sound. "Mighty careless of you, buckskin. How you've lasted so long is a mystery."

"Now what?" Fargo asked.

The prospector raised the Sharps to his shoulder. "Do you really need to ask?"

14

Skye Fargo had learned long ago never to take anyone as they appeared to be. A stranger might smile and be sociable, and the moment Fargo turned his back, plunge a knife into it and steal his poke. A painted warrior bristling with weapons might appear ready to slay any white he came across, yet turn out to be from a friendly tribe. Yet knowing that, Fargo still found the habit hard to break. He'd taken for granted that the old prospector was harmless and now the old man was about to blow out his wick.

"Any last words?" Badger asked.

"You're not the one I'm after. Why shoot me when you don't have to?"

"I like the bonnets and the dresses," Badger said. "I like to fondle them at night."

"You can get them at any dress shop or most any general store," Fargo stalled. His right hand was low at his side and he inched it higher.

"I don't like people, remember? I don't like towns. Every time I go into one, people poke fun at me. Laugh at me behind my back. And now the folks in Haven went and threw me in jail." Badger was growing agitated as he talked and his mouth began to twitch.

"It's stupid to die over a bonnet." Fargo's fingers brushed the bottom of his holster.

"You shouldn't have followed me," Badger said.

"I told you about the missing women." Fargo cupped his

right hand around the middle of his holster and his left hand around his hip.

"They don't mean anything to me."

Fargo nodded at the charnel pit. "You don't care that he chops them up when he's done with them?"

"Why should I? I didn't know any of those folks. To me they're just body parts."

Fargo sighed and slid his right hand up to the grips on his Colt.

"I don't care about the women. I don't care about you. I don't care about anyone but me," Badger said.

"I'll ask you one last time to lower the Sharps." Fargo tensed for the draw. He would sidestep as he shot in case the rifle went off.

"All I care about is gold."

The idea that popped into Fargo's head almost made him smile. Keeping his voice casual he asked, "Have you looked up there?" He nodded toward the black mesa.

Badger looked. The Sharps dipped a couple of inches and he replied, "Why would I want to do that?"

"That's where the townsfolk in Haven say some was found."

"What are you talking about?" Badger asked suspiciously.

"I heard about it from the marshal. There was a man called Wells who found nuggets. He told everyone it was a big strike and he bought provisions and went back out but they never saw him again."

"I never heard of any desert rat named Wells."

"He worked at the livery. Prospected in his spare time. He disappeared about the same time as the first of the women."

Badger blinked and said, "Why, it could have been him who did it."

"The Ghoul?"

Badger nodded. "You saw what's down in that pit. He's killed men before. I bet he killed Wells."

"Why didn't I think of that?"

"Because you ain't clever like me." Badger lowered the Sharps and turned and stared at the mesa. "So that's why he's up there. It's not the women. It's the gold. He wants it for himself."

Fargo took his hand off the Colt. "That's where the Ghoul is?"

"You're awful slow," Badger said. "He has a secret place. I've seen it with my own eyes. I've seen him rubbing the women. He likes to rub and rub as if he can't get enough."

"You'll show me where it is?"

"Find him yourself. All I want is the gold, damn it." Badger walked down to Gladys and snagged the lead rope. "I can't believe I never thought to look up there. All the times I've walked past it, and the times I snuck on up to spy on that fella you're after." He tugged on the rope and led Gladys up the other side. "We never see the nose on our own face."

Fargo was quick to take the Ovaro's reins and hurry after him. It didn't nettle his conscience that he'd lied. It was either that or shoot the old prospector dead. "Wait up."

Badger was pulling the burro as fast as he could walk. "Gold, you said. Nuggets. I wonder did he chip them from a vein or did he find them lying loose?"

"Can you at least tell me where you saw the Ghoul?" Fargo asked. "What part of the mesa?" It would help to narrow it down. The mesa had to be half a mile long and a quarter of mile wide.

"Up it a ways."

"How far up? And on which side? The north? The south? The east? The west?"

"This is the one," Badger said.

"What is?"

"I'm getting too old for this. I need a big strike so I can buy me a cabin somewhere and spend the rest of my days taking it easy in a rocking chair."

Since Fargo had already made up a whopper of a story, he figured it wouldn't hurt to add to it. "I'll make a deal with you."

"Keep your horse. I wouldn't swap Gladys for anything."

"Not that kind of deal," Fargo said. "If you'll tell me exactly where you saw the Ghoul, I'll tell you the rest about Wells."

Badger stopped. "There's more?"

"Wells let drop a hint about where he came across the nuggets," Fargo fibbed. "There's a landmark he mentioned. It might help you find them."

"If that's so, how come no one else has gone after the gold before now?" Badger wanted to know.

"You know how people are. Most townsmen are too scared of hostiles to stray far from town. The farmers can't take the time away from their crops and livestock. Others are just too lazy."

"Are they ever. They expect the gold to jump into their pockets."

"Not everyone has as much grit as you," Fargo told him.

"I have grit?"

"You're out here in the middle of nowhere all by your lonesome. It takes a brave man to do what you do."

"I suppose it does at that." Badger grinned. "I never thought of it like that but being a gold hound ain't for cowards."

By then they were in the mesa's shadow. Badger stopped and said in earnest, "Meeting you was the luckiest day of my life."

Fargo almost felt bad deceiving him.

"Now where is this landmark?" Badger turned toward the mesa. "Point it out."

Fargo scanned the upper reaches. He had his choice of several prominent features. "Do you see that cleft near the top?"

"It reminds me of Andy Jackson's chin."

The remark was so ridiculous that Fargo laughed. "Wells found the nuggets somewhere below it."

Badger beamed happily. "At last. This is the one I've waited my whole life for. I can feel it in my bones." He looked at Fargo. "I don't know how to thank you."

The old prospector's face exploded in a shower of blood and gore and his body arched as taut as a bowstring.

Fargo was in motion as the boom of the shot rolled across the wasteland. He spun and vaulted into the saddle. There in the open, he and the Ovaro were easy targets. He could try to reach the mesa but the rifleman was bound to drop the stallion before they got there and maybe put a slug into him, besides. The only other cover was closer. Reining around, he jabbed his spurs and galloped to the small basin the burro had been concealed in. He went down on the fly as another shot thundered, the slug passing within a whisker of his head. At the bottom he drew rein and swung down. The top of the mesa was visible but he didn't think the shooter was that high up. Still, to be safe, he resorted to a trick he'd taught the stallion—he pulled on the bridle and pushed at a front leg until the Ovaro sank onto its side. He stretched out next to it, his head propped in his hand.

There was another shot, just the one, and a squeal followed by a thud and the clatter of pots, pans and tools.

Fargo took off his hat, set it down, and crabbed to the rim. Unless the man on the mesa had a telescope it was unlikely he would spot him. He dared a peek.

Gladys lay near her dead master. The slug had cored her head and scattered her brains over the hard rock. Her tongue poked from her mouth and a spreading pool of blood was already drawing flies.

Only one of Badger's eyes was still in its socket and that eye was fixed on Fargo. "You should have told me everything at the start," he said to it, and slid to the bottom and put his hat back on. He squinted at the sun. Plenty of daylight left but he wasn't going anywhere. He eased onto his back and slid a hand under his head, and glowered at the world.

The sun crawled across the sky, scorching the earth and the basin and turning the rock into an oven. Fargo felt as if he were being baked alive. The heat got to the Ovaro, too, and twice the stallion tried to rise and each time he held it down and patted it and talked quietly until it settled down.

Fargo had seldom looked forward to a sundown as much as he did to this one. From the rim he watched the western horizon swallow it. The mesa's shadow spread and was in turn swallowed by the darker shadow of advancing night. He didn't move until the first stars sparkled. Then he brought the stallion up off the ground, mounted, and rode up and out the other side of the basin toward the gap through the cliffs.

It was pointless to search the mesa in the dark; the killer would be waiting for him. Fargo figured to rest up and return. He took his time, and by the position of the Big Dipper it was close to midnight when he reached Haven. The town was mostly dark and quiet, with only a few windows aglow. One of those was the parlor window in the boardinghouse. He stripped the Ovaro and went in, the Henry in one hand, his saddlebags over his shoulder. He expected Helsa to be asleep so he was surprised when he saw her in her long robe in the rocking chair, knitting.

She looked up. "Rough day, I take it?"

"I've had better." Fargo set the saddlebags on the settee, wearily sat, and related the death of old Badger.

"That poor crazy man," Helsa said. "And his burro too?"

"There's more." Fargo told her about the charnel pit and regretted it when tears filled her eyes.

"You say you saw the remains of men as well as women? One of them must have been my James."

Fargo hadn't thought of that, and inwardly cursed.

Helsa touched her robe sleeve to the corners of her eyes and composed herself. "The others puzzle me, though. We know of the four women who have disappeared. James would make five. But you saw nine skulls. Who were the other four?"

Fargo shrugged. "Travelers, maybe. Indians. Other prospectors. Who knows?"

"The killer does." Helsa folded up her knitting. "I'd imagine you'll inform Marshal Tibbit in the morning and lead a posse to the black mesa."

"You imagine wrong."

Helsa regarded Fargo as if he were a puzzle. "Why on earth not, may I ask?"

"He's mine."

"Oh, come now. You don't want to see him hung? That is what would happen, you know. No jury would fail to convict him."

"Maybe so," Fargo said.

"But you still want to find him yourself and deal with him as you see fit? Why? Out of spite? For revenge?"

"Call it whatever you want."

"Don't be annoyed with me. I happen to like you. But if you go off alone again, maybe the next time you won't come back. Maybe it's the man on the mesa who kills you and not the other way around."

"Could be," Fargo conceded.

"You're willing to gamble your life to settle a score?"

Fargo felt no need to answer that. He stood and reached for his saddlebags.

"Wait. You must be hungry. I made roast beef for supper and I can heat some up." Helsa came out of the rocking chair and put her hand on his arm. "Please. Let me feed you. I promise to stop trying to persuade you that you're making a mistake."

"In that case," Fargo said, and grinned.

Helsa had kept the stove warm so all she had do was add wood and soon the aroma of the beef and potatoes had Fargo's empty stomach trying to eat itself. She also put coffee on. As she was placing a fork and knife at his elbow she commented, "I almost forgot. Marshal Tibbit has arrested Harvey Stansfield and his two friends."

"Will wonders never cease?"

"I went straightaway to him after you left this morning and reported what they had done. He said enough was enough.

He's thrown them in jail. In the morning he is releasing them with the provision that they leave Haven and never return."

"So that badge of his is good for something besides decorating his shirt," Fargo said.

"That's not quite fair. He does his best."

Fargo let it drop. He had something else on his mind. "How long before the food is done?"

"Oh, five minutes, maybe a little more. Starving, are you?"

Fargo walked over behind her and wrapped his arms around her waist. He pulled her hard against him and cupped her breasts and she stiffened and gasped.

"In more ways than one."

15

Helsa Chatterly turned her face to him, her cheeks dusky with desire.

"Why, handsome sir," she teased. "What is it you have in mind?"

Fargo squeezed her mounds, hard, and she closed her eyes and groaned.

Turning her around, he ground against her and locked his mouth to hers. Her lips yielded; her tongue met his. Her robe easily came undone, and as he had suspected, she had nothing on underneath. Her skin was hot to the touch, her thighs as soft as velvet. He caressed from her knee to her thatch and back down the other leg. Helsa moaned and sucked on his tongue. He felt her hand between his legs, felt her questing fingers find his pole and run up and down. It was almost enough to make him explode.

"Lord, I want you," Helsa breathed in his ear.

Fargo looped his arm under her, lifted her off her feet, and carried her to the kitchen table. She sank back without being asked and pulled at him as he climbed on between her parted legs.

"Yes," Helsa said. "Yes." She fumbled at his belt and his pants. "I want you in me."

Her hunger was mutual. Fargo placed a hand over her bush and ran a finger along her moist slit. She arched her back and her mouth parted in a soundless cry of sensual delight. He smothered it with his own and pinched and pulled on a nipple. Her next moan was into his mouth. A twist of his wrist, and he penetrated her with his middle finger clear to the knuckle. Her bottom came up off the table and she pushed hard against his hand. When they broke the kiss she was panting.

"Don't keep me waiting," Helsa requested.

Fargo didn't intend to. He hiked his gun belt up above his waist, lowered his pants, and ran the tip of his member along her slit. He was going to do it several times but she suddenly raised her bottom and thrust forward and he was buried inside of her.

"Yes," Helsa cooed. "Oh, yes."

Fargo commenced to rock on his knees. The table was hard and his knees soon hurt but the pleasure eclipsed the pain and he continued to impale her. She met each thrust with a thrust of her own, and while his fingers tweaked her breast, her fingers cupped him, down low, and did things that sent pure delight rippling up his spine.

Fargo gripped her hips. He pumped harder and faster and she did the same.

The table swayed and creaked, and it was a wonder the legs didn't collapse.

"I'm close," Helsa cried. "So close."

Not Fargo. He paced himself, letting it build slowly. Suddenly her fingernails dug into his shoulders and she tossed her head from side to side while her body thrashed in the throes of release. He felt her spurt, felt the wet down to his knees.

"Yes! Yes!" Helsa cried.

Fargo might have held off longer except for the smell of the beef and potatoes. He focused on the feel of her, on the moist sensation of her inner sheath, and the next thing he knew, he was spurting. She clutched him close and ground fiercely against him. Her cry mingled with his groan and together they coasted down from the summit of their passion to the hard reality of the kitchen and the table under them.

Helsa kissed him on the mouth. "When you make love to me I feel as if I'm in heaven."

"Hell," Fargo said.

"What's wrong?"

"Don't make more of it than there is." Fargo slid off her, sat up, and swung his legs over the side.

"Don't worry," Helsa said with a hint of reproach. "I'm not about to ask you to marry me."

Fargo's pants were down around his ankles. He bent and pulled them up just as the back door opened and in strode Harvey Stansfield with his six-shooter leveled. Behind him came Dugan and McNee.

Harvey was grinning like the cat that saw the canary in a cage. "Is this a bad time for a visit?" he asked. His mirth was echoed by his friends.

"What's the meaning of this?" Helsa demanded in outrage as she pulled her robe tight around her.

"We came to settle accounts," Harve said, looking at Fargo.

Dugan and McNee had their hands on their revolvers but hadn't drawn them. Both were trying to get an eyeful of Helsa.

"I thought you were in jail."

"That we were, thanks to you," Harvey said. "Bitch." Without warning he took a long step and backhanded her across the face. Helsa fell back against the table and would have fallen except for Fargo, who caught her about the waist.

Helsa was more shocked than hurt. Her hand to her red cheek, she said, "How did you get out?"

Dugan answered her. "It's simple. We told that pudding bowl of a marshal that if he let us loose, we'd pack up and be out of Haven inside of an hour." Dugan chuckled. "Of course, that was five hours ago."

McNee nodded. "Tibbit believed us, the lummox. As if we would leave after what *he* did to us." McNee pointed at Fargo. "Three times he's whupped us but this time is the charm."

"That's right," Harvey gleefully agreed. "We have you now, big man. We have you and we are going to finish what we started."

"Cat got your tongue?" Dugan taunted when Fargo didn't respond.

"I bet he's afraid," McNee said. "He knows we have him dead to rights and he's peeing in his britches."

"Not him," Harve said. "He may be a lot of things but he's not yellow."

"You're standing up for him?" Dugan asked in amazement.

"Hell no. But you didn't hear him beg when we threw that noose around his neck, did you? He hasn't tried to skedaddle when we've jumped him. It's almost a shame he won't live out the night."

"What are you saying?" Helsa said. "You touch a hair on his head and I'll see to it that you are treated to a hemp social, so help me God."

"She will, too," McNee said, sounding worried.

"Not if she's not alive to tell anyone," Dugan said.

Both looked at Harve Stansfield, who shook his head. "Kill a woman and we'll have the whole town after us. But that doesn't mean we let her be a witness."

"A witness to what?" Helsa asked. "To the three of you shooting him down in cold blood?"

"Too quick, too painless," Harve said. "Thanks to him I can barely talk, my lips are so swollen. He has to pay for our bruises and aches."

"But it was *your* fault," Helsa almost shouted. "You tried to hang him even though he was innocent of any wrongdoing."

"How were we to know?" Harve rebutted. "And that's long since water over the dam. All that matters to us is to have our fun and light a shuck before the marshal comes after us."

"Tibbit will throw away the key," Helsa predicted.

"Only if he catches us, and we'll be long gone before they find the body."

Her chin jutting in defiance, Helsa planted herself between Fargo and the three. "I won't let you, you hear? You'll have to go through me to get to him."

"Women," McNee said.

"They are more of a bother than they are worth," Dugan said.

"Except in bed," Harvey chimed in, and leered at her.

Not one of them thought to make Helsa move. Not one of them seemed to realize that they couldn't see Fargo's hands with her standing in front of him.

Fargo realized it. His gun belt was still hitched above his waist, his holster high on his right side. He began to slide his hand toward it.

"Out of the way," Dugan told Helsa.

"No."

"You're trying our patience, lady."

Fargo said over her shoulder, "I have a question."

"I can't wait to hear it," Harve said.

"What *do* you aim to do with me?"

"Damn, you are stupid. What do you think? We aim to drag you out and throw you over a horse and take you into the woods and finish what we started the other night."

Helsa placed a hand to her throat. "You mean you intend to *hang* him? That's hideous."

"He's made us laughingstocks."

Fargo's hand was almost to the holster. He tensed to jerk the Colt but froze when Harve suddenly seized Helsa's wrist and pressed his revolver to her head.

"On second thought we're taking you with us. We leave you here, even trussed up, you might get free and raise a ruckus and we'll have the marshal after us sooner than we want." Harve glanced past her at Fargo and said, "Hell. We forgot to take his pistol, boys." He cocked his. "How about you hand it over nice and easy or this just might go off?"

Fargo would have rather swallowed burning coals than give up the Colt but with that pistol against Helsa's head, he plucked it out.

"McNee, take it and cover him. He's not turning the tables on us this time."

Fargo submitted to having the Colt taken and to having McNee step behind him and jam the muzzle of a six-gun against his spine.

Harvey lowered his pistol and smiled. "Well now. We have the upper hand at last. Dugan, go bring the horses into the backyard."

"Why are you giving all the orders?" Dugan responded. "We're in this the same as you."

They argued, and Helsa shifted toward Fargo and said, "I'm sorry. This is my fault. I should have thrown the bolt on the back door but I wasn't sure if you would come in through the front or the back."

"Hush, bitch," McNee said.

"I can talk if I want," Helsa said. "And don't use that kind of language around me. I'm a lady, I'll have you know."

"Sure you are." McNee laughed. "I saw you on the kitchen table with him, remember? You're as much a whore as any whore I've ever paid for."

Helsa grew so red, she looked fit to burst a blood vessel. "How dare you talk to me like that?"

"Understand this, lady. You mean nothing to me. Harve says we should keep you alive but were it up to me I'd shoot you dead where you stand and not bat an eye."

"You're despicable, all of you."

"We're what?" Harve said. He had finished arguing with Dugan. "Is that any way to talk about the gent who is keeping you alive." He put a hand on her arm. "You should be thankful."

"I can't let you hang him."

"You can't stop us." Harve shoved her toward the back door. Helsa stumbled but recovered.

McNee said, "Your turn, big man," and pushed Fargo at the same time as he rammed his revolver against Fargo's backbone.

Fargo exploded. He whirled and swatted the revolver and slammed a right cross to the chin that rocked McNee onto his heels. Dugan swore and leaped to help, unlimbering his own six-shooter, but he did not quite have it out when Fargo caught him with a looping left to the gut and a hard right to the cheek that sent him crashing into the stove. Harvey spun and took aim and was smirking, confident he had Fargo dead to rights. Harvey didn't count on Helsa jumping onto his back and wrapping an arm around his neck while clawing at his face and eyes with her nails. Howling in pain, Harvey sought to throw her off. Fargo went to help her but McNee was unfurling and raising his revolver. Fargo hit him in the mouth, in the nose, in the right eye; McNee flew backward over the table.

The Colt was at Fargo's feet. Living quicksilver, he dropped to one knee and scooped it up as Dugan pushed clear of the stove. He fired as Dugan pointed his six-shooter, fired as Dugan banged off a shot into the floor, fired a third time and the top of Dugan's head burst.

On the other side of the table, McNee was rising and cursing a mean streak.

He thrust out his six-gun.

Fargo fanned a shot from the hip. At that short a range he didn't need to aim. The lead ripped into McNee's left eye and flipped him around over a chair.

Both hit the floor with a crash.

That left Harvey. Fargo pivoted toward where he had seen him last but only Helsa was there, on the floor, holding her side in pain. The back door slammed.

"Are you all right?" Fargo asked, and when she nodded, he hurtled up and out and into the backyard. The gate was closing. Beyond, a darkling shape was clambering onto a horse. Fargo jerked the Colt up but another horse stepped into his sights.

Harvey Stansfield was fleeing into the night.

Fargo flew to the gate and shoved it open and had to

smack a third horse that got in his way. Springing clear, he raised the Colt. He wanted to be sure. He aimed, and the opportunity was gone; Harve and Harve's mount melted into the darkness. Fargo darted to a bay and in a heartbeat was in the saddle. He gave chase but went only a short way and drew rein. The night had gone quiet save for shouts in Haven. People were wondering what the shots had been about.

Fargo knew what Harvey had done; he had ridden a short distance and stopped to make it harder to locate him. Straining his ears, Fargo rode in a half circle. Nothing. He widened the circle as a commotion rose in town. Again nothing. He was set to sweep farther when Marshal Tibbit shouted.

"Fargo! Can you hear me? I want you back here and I want you back here now!"

Against his better judgment, Fargo returned. The backyard was filled with townsfolk. Helsa was being comforted by several women.

Waiting at the gate was the lawman, in shirtsleeves and looking rumpled.

"There are two dead men inside."

"There would have been three," Fargo said. He swung down and went to walk past.

"I'm afraid I can't turn my back on this," Tibbit said, and gripped his arm. "I'm placing you under arrest."

16

"No," Fargo said. "You're not." There were limits to how much he would abide and Tibbit had crossed the line.

"How is that again?"

"I don't reckon I'll let you arrest me." Fargo crossed the yard toward the back door.

Tibbit overtook him, taking long strides to match his. "Just you hold on a minute. You can't tell a law officer he can't arrest you."

"I just did." Opening the back door, Fargo entered the kitchen and went to the stove. The coffeepot was good and hot.

"But see here. I've been duly appointed to uphold the law." Tibbit tapped his badge to stress the point.

Fargo filled a cup and set the pot back on the stove. He leaned against the table and sipped and then looked at Tibbit, who was impatiently tapping his foot. "You're more worthless than teats on a boar."

"That is quite enough." Tibbit dipped his hand toward the six-gun on his hip.

His arm a blur, Fargo drew the Colt. He had it out and level before Tibbit could touch his. Tibbit blanched and went rigid. With a flourish, Fargo twirled the Colt into his holster. "Don't try that again."

"You wouldn't shoot me."

"Pour yourself a cup and we'll talk."

"I can't," Tibbit said. "I have a weak constitution. It would keep me up all night and I'd be worthless tomorrow." He caught himself. "Worthless. That was your word, wasn't it?"

"I've already been in your jail and I'm not going there again," Fargo set him straight. "I was defending myself. Ask Helsa Chatterly. Those three busted in here and said they were going to hang me. What else was I to do? Yell for help and hope you came?"

"I just don't want more killing," Tibbit said sullenly.

"Tell that to the son of a bitch who has been taking your women, chopping them into pieces, and throwing the pieces in a pit."

"I forgot about him in all the excite—" Tibbit stopped. "Wait. What was that about a pit?"

Fargo told him all that had happened out at the black mesa, concluding with, "I was fixing to come to you in the morning and suggest you gather up a posse. If we head out early enough we can surround the mesa and sweep it from end to end before dark. We're bound to find him."

"I was under the impression you wanted him for yourself."

"Ever been pheasant hunting?"

Tibbit shook his head. "Can't say as I have, no. I've never hunted much. To be honest, I can't stand the blood and the killing. It makes me want to cry."

"Corsets," Fargo said under his breath.

"Sorry?"

"Nothing. What they do is get a bunch of men and walk the fields and flush the birds into taking wing and the hunter who is nearest shoots it."

Tibbit was quiet a bit. "I see. You're hoping we'll flush him and you can shoot him."

Fargo shrugged. "It could be me. It could be any of you."

"You're forgetting something." Tibbit drew himself up to his full height. "I am obligated to go by the letter of the law and the law says I must try to take him alive to stand trial for his crimes."

"Come down out of the clouds, Marion," Fargo said. It was the first time he had used the lawman's first name.

"Excuse me?"

"The man on that mesa won't let you take him alive. He'll fight, he'll fight hard, and it could be some of your posse won't come back."

"If there are enough of us he'll realize it's pointless and might surrender." Tibbit brightened at the notion. "Why, I'll round up every able-bodied man in town and send for the closest farmers. I can raise forty men or better."

"You do what you want."

Tibbit regarded him thoughtfully. "You don't like me very much, do you, Mr. Fargo?"

"I like you fine. It's your stupid I don't care for."

"My what?"

"When you do what you shouldn't."

"But who is to say I'm wrong and you're right?"

"That's what stupid people always say."

A flush spread from Tibbit's neck to his hairline. "I don't like being insulted, sir. I don't like it at all." He tromped to the hall, and paused. "I'll have a posse ready to ride out at dawn. One way or the other, this whole mess will end."

"We hope," Fargo said.

"It's your plan yet you sound pessimistic. He's one man. We'll have forty or more. He's as good as caught."

"There you go again." Fargo swallowed more coffee. "This man is smart. He's picked a good hiding place. And he's a good shot."

"Forty to one," Tibbit emphasized.

"That won't make a difference to him. He'll be like a cornered wolf up there. A cornered *rabid* wolf. And you can never tell what a rabid animal will do."

"He'll surrender or he will die. It's that simple." Tibbit touched his hat brim and turned to go.

"Aren't you forgetting something?" Fargo asked.

"Not that I can think of."

Fargo pointed at the two bodies.

"Oh. Mercy me. Yes, I suppose it wouldn't do to leave them there. Helsa wouldn't like that at all."

It took half an hour for the lawman to organize a handful of men to carry the bodies out and wipe up the blood.

Fargo stayed in the kitchen drinking coffee. Helsa Chatterly came in, her arms wrapped around her bosom, and moved tiredly to the pitcher and poured a glass of water.

"I'm glad that's over."

"It's not," Fargo said.

"You mean Harvey Stansfield? Surely he won't try again."

"He'll want me dead more than ever," Fargo predicted.

"I hope you're wrong." Helsa drank and set the glass down and bowed her head. "I'm going to turn in. How about you?"

"I'll be up in a minute."

She came over and kissed him on the cheek. "I'm sorry you had to shoot them."

"I'm not."

"You don't mean that. You took two lives. Surely that will haunt you the rest of your days."

Fargo had lost count of the number of lives he'd taken; he never gave another thought to any of them. Most were like the pair tonight, out to do him violence or to hurt someone else, and had to be stopped. In his book they deserved what they got, and good riddance. He didn't tell her that. He said, "Get a good night's rest and you'll feel better in the morning."

"Good night, handsome." Helsa padded off.

Fargo finished his coffee. He bolted the front and back doors. He went from window to window, checking that they were latched. He blew out the lamp in the parlor and climbed the stairs to his room. Instead of stripping and climbing into bed, he took a pillow and placed it vertically under the blankets to give the illusion of someone sleeping. Then he blew out the bedroom lamp, stretched out on the floor with his

124

back to a wall, and fell asleep with his arm for a pillow and his Colt in his hand.

A faint pink hue marked the eastern sky when Fargo awoke. Sitting up, he stretched and slid the Colt into his holster and put his hat on. He quietly went downstairs and out into the early-morning chill of the new day. Well before the sun was up he was in the saddle in front of the marshal's office. He was the first one there.

A golden crown glowed bright when Tibbit showed. He had bags under his eyes and his clothes were a mess. He nodded at Fargo and went into his office. Fargo followed and claimed a chair while the lawman put a fresh pot of coffee on the stove.

"I got the word out," Tibbit said. "I should have over forty men here by daybreak."

"It already *is* daybreak," Fargo pointed out. "And no one else is here."

"Give them time."

The sun was all the way up when Felicity's father and several of his friends arrived. Then it was Myrtle's father, Joseph, and some of his friends. In all, over two dozen gathered and talked in hushed tones until Marshal Tibbit emerged.

"Men, I want to thank you for coming. I'm expecting more so we'll wait for them to get here."

Fargo leaned against the jamb. "We should leave now."

"What's your rush?" Tibbit asked.

"It's a big mesa. We'll need most of the day to search."

"Forty can search faster than twenty," Tibbit said. "I say we give them another hour."

Reluctantly, Fargo gave in. They needed him to guide them and he needed them to scour every square yard of the mesa. It was eight before most of those Tibbit was counting on got there, and eight thirty before they were finally shed of Haven.

Fargo rode at the head with Tibbit and Tom Wilson, the townsman who had tried to stop the lynching that night on the trail. In a short while Sam Worthington joined them, the big farmer saying, "I thought you should know, Marshal. Some of the men are saying as how we should shoot the Ghoul on sight."

"I made it clear he is to be taken into custody," Tibbit said, with a pointed glance at Fargo.

"Myrtle's pa doesn't agree and he's worked up the others," the farmer revealed. "I can't hardly blame them. If my Melissa was to vanish, I'd feel the same way."

"Doesn't anyone know the difference between right and wrong anymore?" Tibbit asked. "Damn it, Sam. Why am I wearing this badge if no one ever listens to me?"

The farmer didn't reply.

"Go back with the others. Spread the word that I won't put up with any shenanigans. Anyone bucks me on this will be thrown in jail."

"I'll do as you want but it won't make any difference."

"Why not?"

"I expect you already know."

"Say it anyway. I want to hear."

Worthington met Fargo's eye, and frowned. "No one takes you serious, Marion. You threaten and you bluster but you never really do anything unless you're forced to."

"That's harsh."

"You asked," Worthington said. "And while I'm at it, I might as well let you know that there has been talk of going to the town council and demanding the council replace you."

Tibbit couldn't hide his surprise. "After all I've done for these people, they would turn on me?"

"That's just it," Worthington said. "What *have* you done except wear the badge? I'm not one of the ones who wants you to give it up, mind you, but they think you are worthless."

"Where have I heard that before?" Tibbit said bitterly, with another pointed look at Fargo.

"Sorry to be the one to break the news." Worthington reined around.

"A fine 'how do you do?'" Tibbit said in disgust. He turned to Wilson. "How about you, Tom? Are you with me or against me?"

"I'm for Haven."

"That's no answer."

"Then let me spell it out for you," Wilson said. "I'm for anything that makes the town a better place to live. Right now, a lawman worth his salt is what we need most."

"Not you too?"

"You're just not cut out for it, Marion. You're good at corsets. You're not so good at keeping the peace."

"Other than the women disappearing, there hasn't been anything I couldn't handle."

"You didn't stop Harvey Stansfield and his two friends from assaulting Mr. Fargo, here."

"Several times," Fargo said.

"I had them in jail."

"And let them out," Wilson said.

"Only because they promised me."

"They what?"

"They promised they would behave and I believed them. You can't fault someone for trusting their fellow man."

Wilson lifted his reins. "I think I'll go back and ride with Sam and the others."

"Fine. Be that way." Tibbit shifted in his saddle toward Fargo. "Do you believe this?"

"Yes."

"Hell in a basket. Everyone is against me. But you wait. They'll change their minds after we catch the Ghoul." Tibbit took off his hat and swatted it against his leg and put it back on again. "If it's the last thing I do, I'll make them take me seriously. I'll show them a man can be a good corset salesman and a good lawman, both."

"Just so you don't get anyone killed," Fargo said.

17

The black mesa towered stark and remote in the dark heart of the cloud-covered wasteland. The wind was bringing a storm from the west and thunderheads framed the far horizon. Vivid flashes rent the black clouds, so far away that the consequent thunder was the faintest of rumbles.

"Just what we need," Marshal Tibbit complained.

Fargo wasn't happy about it either. They had half a mile to cover and the dust their mounts raised could be seen for three or four. The Ghoul was bound to have spotted them and would either be long gone or prepared to spill a lot of blood. Neither prospect was appealing.

To add to Fargo's unease, the townsmen and farmers were much too lax.

They wouldn't stop gabbing about everything from the weather to their families. It got so, he began to wonder if any of them fully realized what they were up against.

"Maybe we should turn around and come back tomorrow," Tibbit suggested.

"We came this far," Fargo said, implying it would be a shame not to finish it. Tippet took it another way.

"I'm not yellow, if that's what you're thinking."

"I never said . . ." Fargo began.

"I'll show you." Tibbit rose in the stirrups and faced the posse. "We need to hurry, men, to beat that storm. At a gallop, if you would!" And he whooped and used his spurs.

"No!" Fargo shouted, but the rest were quick to follow the

lawman's lead and went pounding past, many yipping and hollering as if it were some sort of child's game, all save for Sam Worthington who stopped next to the Ovaro.

"What's the matter?"

"The fools," Fargo said, and lit out after them. They were charging across open land in plain sight. He dreaded what might happen.

The shod hooves of the posse's mounts raised thunder of their own. They spread out, Marshal Tibbit at the center urging them on with waves of his arm.

They were caught up in the charge, oblivious to all else including Fargo's shouts for them to stop.

The black mesa seemed to grow as Fargo drew nearer, an illusion enhanced by the darkening clouds that mantled it in shadow.

"Stop, damn you! You're riding into his gun sights!"

Marshal Tibbit was whooping the loudest of all and lashing his horse with the reins.

To the west lightning split the sky and real thunder boomed.

It explained why Fargo didn't hear the first shot. The posse was two hundred yards from the base of the mesa when a rider next to Tibbit threw up his arms and catapulted off his saddle and was nearly trampled by the horse behind him. Tibbit didn't notice and kept going but a few others did and drew rein.

Fargo heard the second shot. A man in a bowler lost part of his face and fell headlong to the ground. The third shot lifted a farmer clear of his mount, a scarlet stain in the middle of his shirt. The fourth shot brought down a horse. By then the rest awakened to their peril. They broke right and left, some heading back the way they had come, others racing for the mesa, and cover.

Fargo galloped for the mesa. He listened to the rifle bang three more times before it went empty. A Spencer, he suspected, since Spencers held seven shots.

Two more bodies joined those already down.

Tibbit's hat had been whipped off and he was riding bareheaded and bawling for everyone to follow him. A handful did. The rest made for boulders and patches of vegetation.

Maybe twenty, all told, reached the mesa, Fargo among them. He clattered into a stand of trees and drew rein. Worthington and another man were right behind them. Together they swung down, shucked their rifles, and moved to trees.

The Spencer was still silent but Fargo wasn't fooled. It took only seconds to reload. The Ghoul was waiting for them to show themselves.

"What do we do?" asked the townsman with Worthington, his eyes wide with fear.

"We stay put."

"But he's killed a bunch of us."

"Listen to Mr. Fargo, Timothy," Sam Worthington said. "He knows what he's doing."

Timothy half rose from concealment. "So do I. I've hunted bear and deer. I'm going up whether you two are or not." He took a step and his left cheek dissolved in a shower of blood and flesh.

Fargo dived to pull him to the ground but it was already too late; the exit wound was as big around as an apple. He rolled aside as the body crashed down and took up his position behind the tree.

"Tim always did think he knew better than other folks," Sam Worthington said.

Fargo scoured the slope for sign of the others. They had all gone to ground and were well hid. Then a hatless head popped out from behind a boulder and Marshal Tibbit waved.

"Fargo! I'm over here! Do you see him?"

Fargo motioned for him to get down. "I am surrounded by amateurs," he remarked.

"Most of us push plows or pencils," Sam Worthington said. "We're not man-killers."

The bodies sprinkled over the wasteland were a testament to

the farmer's statement. Fargo almost regretted involving them. "Cover me the best you can," he directed.

"What are you fixing to do?"

Fargo made sure a cartridge was in the Henry's chamber.

"The Ghoul will pick you off the moment you step into the open," the farmer remarked.

"He'll try." Fargo sank onto his belly and crawled to Timothy. He had to lift and tug to get the jacket off. Then, holding it in his left hand, he crawled to the last tree.

Worthington reached the next trunk over. "I'll spray some lead to discourage him but without knowing where he is it might not help much."

"Take care of my horse until I get back." Fargo tossed the jacket into the open. The Spencer blasted, and simultaneously he pumped his legs for a cluster of boulders forty feet higher. The Spencer cracked again and a dirt geyser spewed next to his foot. Behind him the big farmer commenced shooting as rapidly as he could. A slug clipped a whang from Fargo's buckskin shirt. Another nicked his hat. He dived and rolled and was up running and bounded the last few yards with his skin prickling.

Fargo flattened behind a boulder. He was caked with sweat. He looked at Worthington and held his thumb up. Worthington grinned and ducked behind the tree.

The next moment, to Fargo's complete and utter amazement, Marshal Tibbit started up the slope after him. Worse, as Tibbit burst from concealment he shouted loud enough for all creation—and the Ghoul—to hear.

"Here I come! Cover me!"

Fargo swore and heaved up and fired shot after shot. The Spencer answered. Fargo sent four swift blasts at puffs of gun smoke he spotted and the Spencer fell silent.

Tibbit gained a nearby boulder and sank to his knees, rasping for breath. "Thanks," he puffed.

"You're a damned fool."

"Here now," Tibbit said. "Don't start."

Fargo studied the slope above them. It wasn't as steep as it had appeared to be but climbing it would take some doing and he would have to cross a lot of open space.

"I've done pretty good so far," Tibbit remarked.

"Besides getting six or seven men shot?" Fargo said. There might be more. He hadn't counted them.

"How you can blame that on me, I fail to see."

Fargo stared at him.

"Why do you keep doing that?"

From the west scuttled the thunderhead. The wind grew stronger, so strong it pushed at Fargo's hat. The scent of rain was heavy in the air. Flashes of lightning lit the roiling clouds and now and then a bolt streaked to earth.

Tibbit sat with his back to the boulder and began reloading his revolver.

"That was a glorious charge, wasn't it? I only wish so many hadn't turned tail."

"They were the smart ones," Fargo said.

"How can you say that? You, of all people?" Tibbit started to insert a cartridge the wrong way and reversed it so it slid into the chamber. "The Ghoul must be brought to bay for his misdeeds and today is the day we do it."

"He has uncommon luck."

"Why?"

Fargo nodded at the ever darkening heavens.

"The storm will help us as much as him. We can sneak up on him under cover of the rain and capture him."

"You hope."

"Must you always dwell on the worst that can happen?" Tibbit finished reloading and cocked the six-shooter. Cupping his other hand to his mouth, he hollered down, "Men, listen to me! As soon as the rain starts we are going up after him. I'll give a yell. That will be the signal. Stay close together, and each man watch the other's back." He grinned at Fargo. "How was that?"

"The Ghoul heard that, too."

"So? We outnumber him. He's had the better of us so far but now we'll get the better of him." Tibbit chuckled and rubbed his badge with his sleeve. "I do so love this job."

"You're a wonderment," Fargo said.

"Thank you."

Wet drops struck Fargo's face. Lightning crackled, close enough to illuminate half the mesa, and the thunder that followed buffeted his eardrums. When it faded he said, "Do you know a man named Timothy?"

"Tim Bainbridge? Yes. I know him well. He came to Haven about four months ago. He works as a clerk. He has a pretty young wife and a new baby. They are a fine family."

"When you get back break the news to her and her baby that her husband was shot in the face."

"Why would you say a thing like that?" Tibbit demanded. "Of course I'll tell her. But why?"

"Figure it out yourself."

"You know," Marshal Tibbit said, "I am beginning to regret asking you for help. You prick at me like an itch I can't scratch."

"Someone has to," Fargo said.

"You make it sound as if I can't do anything."

"You can sell corsets."

"You chew a bone to death. Do you know that? When we get back I would be grateful if you would pack up and leave."

"When I'm damn good and ready."

More drops fell, large cold drops, and then the sky opened up and down came the deluge. The wind howled. The lightning was near continuous, the thunder near constant.

Fargo darted around the boulder and climbed. He barely heard Tibbit yell for him to stop. The flashes of lightning lit the terrain but the rain was so heavy the Ghoul would have to be ten feet away to spot him. At the next boulder he paused. Bellowing told him Tibbit and the rest of the posse had started up after him. He resumed his ascent.

The wind howled and keened. The footing became treacherous. Twice Fargo slipped and went down on one knee. He kept a firm grip on the Henry. The slope steepened and he used his free hand for extra purchase. He was soon soaked to the skin and had to repeatedly wipe his sleeve across his face to keep the rain out of his eyes.

A shot cracked. Not from above but from below. A nervous posse member, Fargo reckoned. He hoped the man hadn't been shooting at him.

Up and up and up he went, the wind pummeling him. He almost lost his hat but snatched it in time to jam it back on. He lowered his head against the rain and pistoned higher and suddenly the ground seemed to fall away under him and he tripped and nearly fell. Crouching, he tried to make sense of it and realized he had come to a flat shelf, invisible from below. The next bolt of lightning showed that it went a good long way in both directions and for forty or fifty feet in.

Pulling his hat brim as low as it could go to ward off the rain, Fargo slowly advanced. He had a hunch this was where the Ghoul had been firing from. He went maybe twenty feet when he saw what he took to be a boulder about as big as a watermelon. A bolt from above blazed the shelf white with light and in the glare he saw that it wasn't a boulder at all.

Fargo crouched and bent lower and his skin crawled as if with a thousand ants.

It was a woman's head. Most of the flesh had long since rotted and her skin had withered. Her hair was plastered to what was left of her face and down over the sides of her skull. She had died with her mouth agape in a twisted scream.

Fargo gripped the hair and turned the head so the face was to the ground. Wiping his hand on his pants, he edged forward. More lightning revealed a cliff that he took to be solid stone until he discerned the black maw of what might be a cave.

The Ghoul's lair, Fargo suspected. He wedged the Henry's stock to his shoulder. Staying low, he moved each foot with care. He was at the cave opening when his foot bumped something. He glanced down and his skin did more crawling. The thing he had bumped was a withered hand, possibly from the same woman.

Fargo looked up just as lightning streaked the firmament. A dozen feet in stood a figure.

There was only one person it could be.

Fargo had found the Ghoul.

18

Fargo trained the Henry on the center of the figure and curled his finger around the trigger. Another instant and he would have fired. But something about the figure gave him pause. He waited for the next bolt to light up the shelf, and when it did, he slowly straightened. As wary as a cougar, he moved into the cave.

It smelled of food odors and woodsmoke and human sweat. He was close enough now that the next flash confirmed what he thought he had seen—the figure had long flowing hair and its arms and legs were outspread. More bolts revealed more details: the blackened embers of a fire; a mess of blankets; a shovel and an ax; the haunch of a deer; a lantern, and beside it a box of lucifers. Hunkering, he soon had the lantern lit.

In its glow Fargo saw the figure clearly. She was young, barely twenty, and as naked as the day she had been born. Her wrists and ankles were bound to poles imbedded in the cave floor. Her head hung low, her hair half over her face, and her eyes were closed. Either she was unconscious or she was dead. A gag suggested the former.

Fargo raised the lantern higher. The cave went back another ten feet and ended at a rock wall. Lying over near the right wall were female undergarments and a pair of shoes. The woman's, he suspected. He went up to her, set the lantern down, and lightly touched a finger to her throat. There was a pulse, weak but steady. He was lowering his hand when her eyelids fluttered and her eyes slowly opened. They were dull and vacant.

"Are you Myrtle Spencer?"

At the sound of his voice she stiffened and stark terror wiped away the dullness. She mewed in fear and weakly tugged at the ropes. Her wrists and ankles, he saw, were caked with dried blood.

"It's all right. I'm here to help you."

The woman stopped mewing and blinked. Tears started to flow and she quaked from head to toe.

"Where is the man who did this to you?" Fargo asked. "Where is the Ghoul?"

The woman went on quaking. Her tears went on flowing.

Fargo set down the Henry and drew the Arkansas toothpick from his ankle sheath. "I'll have you down in a moment." He cut the rope on her right ankle and then on her left, careful not to cut her. Rising, he sliced the rope on her left wrist and she sagged and would have collapsed if he hadn't hooked an arm around her to support her. She was still quaking. He cut the rope on her right wrist and she fell against him. With great care he carried her to the blankets and went to lay her on them.

Myrtle Spencer, if that is who she was, looked down and broke into violent convulsions. She shrieked and struck at his chest and kicked but she was so weak he hardly felt the blows. Baffled, he drew back.

"What's the matter? I need to put you down."

The woman grew still. But when he went to lay her on the blankets she whimpered and kicked. At last he understood. Backing away from the blankets, he eased her to the ground. She didn't resist. He pried at the gag but the knots were so tight he had to resort to the toothpick. "Are you Miss Spencer?"

She stared at him without answering. Or, rather, past him, at the roof of the cave.

"Myrtle Spencer?" Fargo tried once more.

The vacant quality was in her eyes. They lacked any spark of vitality whatsoever.

"I'm with a posse. We're after the Ghoul."

She might as well have been on another world.

"Do you know where he got to?"

Nothing.

"Would you like water or food?"

Nothing at all.

Fargo stood and brought the undergarments over and with a lot of lifting and him doing all the work, he slipped a chemise over her head and shoulders and pulled it down as low as it would go. He had just finished and stepped back when Marshal Tibbit bellowed.

"A cave, by God, boys!"

Boots thudded and scraped.

Into the cave rushed Joseph Spencer. He came to Fargo's side, and groaned. His face was pale as a sheet. "Myrtle, honey? It's your pa."

She showed no more life than she had with Fargo.

"Didn't you hear me?" Joseph knelt and gently clasped her hand. "You're safe now, girl."

Fargo was aware of other men ringing them. Tibbit was on his left, dripping wet and grinning.

"We found her! We actually found her. This will show everyone I'm not worthless."

Fargo almost hit him.

"Myrtle?" Joseph touched her cheek and her brow. "What's wrong with her? Why won't she say anything?"

"Could be she's in shock," a man said.

"Could be she's been scared out of her mind," said another.

"Myrtle?" Joseph lightly shook her shoulders but all she did was go on staring her eerie empty stare. "God, no."

"Where's the Ghoul?" a townsman asked, and the rest of

the men began moving about the cave searching when it was plain he wasn't there.

Marshal Tibbit beamed at Fargo. "You did it. You said you would find him and you did. We're all in your debt, me most of all."

"It's not over," Fargo said.

Outside, the storm was abating. The rain had reduced to a drizzle and the lightning flashes were fewer and farther between.

"Did you see the Ghoul? Did you get a good look at him?"

Fargo shook his head.

"Well, he can't have gotten far. We'll get him yet. With your help he's as good as caught."

Fargo could have pointed out that the rain had washed away any tracks.

He reclaimed the Henry and went to the cave mouth. The worst of the thunderhead was to the east and the clouds overhead had gone from black to gray.

Sam Worthington came over and stood staring into the drizzle. "He's gotten clean away, hasn't he?"

"He has," Fargo said.

"Damn." The big farmer looked over his shoulder. "That poor girl. She's a friend of my daughter's. You should have known her. Always so sweet and kind and forever smiling." He ran a callused hand across his brow. "What could he have done to her?"

"You know as well as I do."

"Yes. Yes, I suppose I do. I just don't want to admit it. It goes against everything that is decent in this world. I don't understand how a thing like this can happen."

"Ask God," Fargo said.

The farmer scowled. "That's a terrible thing to say. The parson would call it blasphemy."

"Have the parson ask Myrtle Spencer how she feels."

Worthington looked at him and said, not without admiration, "You're a hard man."

"It's a hard life."

Marshal Tibbit bustled over looking as happy as if he had just eaten a fresh-baked apple pie. "We can't get a word out of her but I bet the doc can." He scanned the wet wasteland and nudged Fargo. "The rain has about stopped. How soon can you head out after the Ghoul?"

"He's long gone."

"He can't have more than half an hour start on us," Tibbit said. "Forty minutes at the most. Find which direction he took and me and five or six others will go with you. The rest are taking Myrtle back to town."

"I'll look around," Fargo said. Now that he thought about it, there hadn't been any sign the Ghoul kept his mount in the cave. It had to be elsewhere. He hiked to the north end of the shelf. The slope beyond was too steep for a horse. He walked to the south and was thirty feet past the cave when he spied a game trail leading toward the crest. Made, no doubt, by whatever used the cave before the Ghoul moved in. Fargo headed up, the footing treacherous on the wet rocks. In spots the climb was almost sheer. Eventually he gained the summit and found what he was looking for: a stake and a rope.

Essentially flat, the top of the mesa was sprinkled with brush and boulders. The ground was mostly dirt, not rock. Old tracks, extremely faint but not entirely washed away, pointed to the south.

Fargo turned and hurried down the mesa to the Ovaro. As he was crossing the shelf someone called his name.

Most of the posse had gathered outside the cave, apparently waiting for Joseph Spencer and his daughter.

Marshal Tibbit had spotted him and came over. "Where are you off to in such a rush?"

"With luck I can end this by nightfall." Fargo continued walking, forcing the lawman to keep up if he wanted to keep talking.

"What do you mean by end it?"

"Don't play stupid."

Tibbit gripped his arm. "Hold on. Why must I keep repeating myself? If we can, we're to take the Ghoul into custody."

"If *you* can," Fargo said.

"Damn it. You're the most pigheaded individual I've ever met. You can't go around killing people because you feel like it."

"The Ghoul does."

"But you're not him!" Tibbit exclaimed in exasperation. "You are obligated by law to take him alive."

"Your law, not mine."

Tibbit puffed out his cheeks in anger. "You're a citizen of the United States, are you not? As such, you are under her jurisdiction, and the law of the land is that you can't go around killing folks because they cross you or you blame them for nearly being lynched."

"Save the speech."

Marshal Tibbit jerked on Fargo's arm. "Goddamn you. No one is above the law. Not me, not you, not anyone."

Fargo patted his Colt. "Out here the only law is this."

"I refuse to bandy words. If you go after the Ghoul you're to bring him back alive if it is at all possible. I mean it."

Fargo looked at him. "You don't get it yet, do you?"

"Get what?"

"You never mean anything. You have no more backbone than mud."

"That's not true."

Fargo pulled his arm from the lawman's grasp and was over the side before Tibbit could object.

By now the storm was miles away. Here and there a golden shaft pierced the clouds. Fargo came to the stand and climbed on the Ovaro and descended to the bottom of the mesa. He rode to the south and was at the extreme southern end when his face lit with a smile. "Got you," he said.

The tracks were so fresh some had rainwater in the bottom. They came down off the mesa and went off across the wasteland, passing close to the charnel pit. Fargo averted his face and held his breath until he was well past it.

Save for the clink of the Ovaro's hooves and the creak of Fargo's saddle, silence reigned. Again and again he rose in the stirrups but he failed to spot his quarry.

The clouds broke apart and the sun shone steady, as hot as ever. Steam rose from the ground and the air shimmered to invisible waves. In no time the puddles had burned away and the land looked as parched and barren as ever.

So far off they were stick figures, Fargo spotted a man on a horse. He brought the Ovaro to a trot. Soon the distance narrowed. He slowed after a while to spare the stallion but he chafed at the need.

The wasteland gave way to forest. By Fargo's reckoning he was ten to twelve miles west of Haven. He found the Ghoul's tracks easily enough and was surprised to discover that the Ghoul had turned east. He'd figured the killer would stay away from human habitation but it appeared that the Ghoul was in fact making a beeline for town. At first it made no sense. Why would the Ghoul risk being lynched? Fargo wondered. Then it hit him. No one knew who the Ghoul was. The killer could mingle with the townsfolk with no one the wiser.

Fargo rode faster but it was several hours after sundown when he finally reached the outskirts. He lost the tracks in the jumble of prints in the main street, and swore.

Fargo doubted the posse had returned yet. Haven lay quiet and deceptively peaceful under the stars. Two men were talking in front of the livery and an older woman was enjoying the night air in a chair on her front porch. Those were the only people he saw.

Fargo went to the boardinghouse. He tied the Ovaro to the picket fence and walked up the steps to the front door. He didn't knock. He was about to take the stairs to his room when he heard voices in the parlor. One was Helsa's. Thinking she might be willing to fix him a meal, he walked down the hall and stopped in the doorway.

Helsa was in the rocking chair, her knitting in her lap. She had a strange expression on her face and appeared almost as white as her picket fence, as if all the blood had drained from her body. The skin under her eyes glistened with recently shed tears. On seeing him she gave a tiny shake of her head as if to suggest he was intruding.

"I thought I heard you talking to someone."

"You did," said a male voice, and a man rose from behind the rocking chair with a Spencer in his hands. He wore a black hat and a black jacket and was in need of a shave. "Permit me to introduce myself," he said with exaggerated politeness. "Most everyone hereabouts calls me the Ghoul."

19

Fargo made no move to draw his Colt. He would be shot dead before he cleared leather. He looked at Helsa and then at the Ghoul, trying to figure out why the Ghoul had come here, of all places, and then he noticed that the Ghoul was about her age and what women would call handsome and had piercing blue eyes.

"Oh, hell."

Helsa coughed and said hoarsely, "Mr. Fargo, I'd like you to meet my husband, James Chatterly."

"Your dead husband," Fargo said.

"I thought he was," Helsa said softly. "All this time I've been in misery, and it was a ruse."

James Chatterly grinned. "A damned clever ruse, my dear, you'll have to admit." He stepped clear of the rocking chair, the muzzle of the Spencer fixed squarely on Fargo.

"You've been taking the young women," Fargo said.

"I've been taking the younger women," James Chatterly echoed.

"And others when you find them."

"And others when I find them, yes. Once I started I couldn't stop. It felt too good."

Helsa cleared her throat. "What did?"

"Can't you guess, my dear? What did we like to do more than anything else? What couldn't I get enough of?"

"God, no."

"God, yes," James Chatterly said. "It started with Felicity.

She was a little tart, that one. We were fooling around behind your back. When you went shopping she'd come over. It went on for over a year, until one day she came to me and said it had to stop."

"I don't want to hear this," Helsa said.

Her husband ignored her. "I didn't want it to. I liked making love to her. I liked it so much I was in a funk for weeks until it occurred to me how I could go on having her any hour of the day or night for as long as I cared to."

"No, no, no," Helsa said.

James turned to Fargo. "I used to hunt, you see. One day I came across the mesa and decided to explore. That's when I found the cave. I remembered it when I had my brainstorm. It was perfect."

Helsa bowed her head and tears flowed. She cried quietly, with only an occasional sniffle, as her husband went on.

"I couldn't just disappear. Folks would have been suspicious. So I cut my arm and left blood on my saddle to give the idea I had been killed. I had another horse no one knew about, one I'd bought from a man passing through Haven, and I went off to the cave and spent the next several months satisfying myself with Felicity." He paused. "Then a peculiar thing happened."

"You lost interest in her," Fargo guessed.

"How did you know?" James Chatterly nodded. "Maybe it was just that it was me and her and no one else for days and weeks on end. I wanted someone new. So I got rid of her and snuck close to town and helped myself to a new woman."

Helsa choked down a sob. "How could you?" she forlornly asked.

"Now, now," James said.

"How could you?" Helsa practically screamed. "All those years we were together, I wasn't good enough for you? You secretly hankered after other women?"

"After younger ones, yes. After women who were like you were when we first met."

"Oh, James."

"Don't."

"What you did was *wrong*."

"I saw it as setting myself free to do as I'd always longed to do. I could make love any hour of the day or night in any way I wanted and there was nothing they could do." James chuckled. "For me it was heaven and then some."

"Those poor girls," Helsa said.

"Yes. Those girls. With their young, ripe bodies. With their lips and their breasts. I couldn't get enough. I'd run my hands over their silky skin for hours at a time. I did more than make love to those girls. I worshipped them."

"And chopped them up when you were tired of them," Fargo mentioned.

"What?" Helsa said.

James Chatterly shrugged. "I had to dispose of the bodies somehow and the ground was too hard to dig graves. So I took my ax and gave them forty whacks and threw them in that pit I found."

"You didn't," Helsa declared.

"It was no different from breaking the neck of a chicken or putting down a dying dog."

Helsa's moist eyes mirrored her horror. "To think I once loved you. To think I once thought you were the best man who ever lived."

"You're being dramatic."

Grasping a knitting needle, Helsa started to rise out of the rocking chair but sat back down.

Fargo asked James Chatterly, "What are you doing here?"

"That's your doing."

"Mine?"

"I took a shot at you in the woods and tried to drop you at the pit but you got away. You tracked me down. You brought the posse to the cave and I was forced to run. Now I must go somewhere else and start all over again. But first I wanted to see my wife again." James smiled at Helsa. "I wanted to say good-bye."

146

"You vile, despicable brute."

"No name-calling, if you please. It's most unbecoming."

"You're insane. Stark raving insane."

James Chatterly sighed. "I didn't expect you would understand. You have always lived your life by what others do and not by what you want to do."

"Listen to yourself," Helsa said. "Standing there so calmly and talking as if we were discussing the weather when we are talking about rape and murder."

"Don't forget the beating and the whipping," James said with a smirk. "I am fond of that part."

"God help you."

"That's another thing I've learned," James said. "All those years I lived in fear of something that isn't." He laughed and looked at each of them and squared his shoulders. "I reckon that's about all there is worth saying. Time to finish this and be on my way."

"Surely you're not going to harm *me*?" Helsa said.

"Surely I am."

"But why? What did I ever do but love you and care for you and feed you and nurse you when you were sick?"

"That you did," James acknowledged. "You were as good a wife as a man ever had. You just weren't ever enough of the other."

"What other? The sex thing? Did I ever refuse you? Did I ever once kick you out of my bed?"

Fargo deliberately stayed quiet in the hope they would forget he was there. It seemed to be working. James was focused on Helsa and only on Helsa. He shifted his weight to the balls of his feet, and tensed.

"No, you did not," James was telling her. "You were more willing than most wives. I'll give you that. And at one time I did love you."

"And I loved you," Helsa said softly.

"But that's the past and this is now. You know what I must do, don't you, now that I have confided in you?"

Fargo was ready to spring. He would dive into the hall past the doorway.

Chatterly would shoot but the wall would shield him from the slugs. Or so he hoped. Then a hard object was jammed low against his back and a voice whispered behind his head.

"Not one twitch or I blow you to hell."

Neither James nor Helsa had noticed. They were looking at each other. James was smiling. Helsa appeared shocked.

"You wouldn't," she said. "Not to me. Not to your own wife."

"Female is female," James replied. "You're no different from any other. I will at least make it quick, out of respect for what we once had."

"I can't believe this."

"Believe it, my dear. Life is nothing if not unpredictable. Look at me. Would you ever have imagined I would be as I am?"

The man behind Fargo stepped past Fargo into the parlor with his rifle trained on James Chatterly. "That's enough gab out of you two. Drop that Spencer, mister, or die where you stand."

"Harvey Stansfield!" Helsa blurted.

James possessed superb self-control. He stood stock-still and regarded the intruder with puzzlement. "Stansfield? I remember that name."

"Who the hell are you?" Harve responded. "And drop that damn rifle now or I'll shoot."

Instead of letting go, James tucked at the knees and set the Spencer on the floor. "Don't you recognize me?"

"Mister, I never set eyes on—" Harve stopped. "Wait a second. But you can't be him. He's dead."

"I feel very alive at the moment," James said. "Where is the rest of the posse? Have they surrounded the house?"

"Posse?" Harve responded. "What the hell are you talking about? They've got a posse out after me?"

It was Helsa who answered. "No. Marshal Tibbit has one out after him." She pointed at James.

"What on earth for?"

"He's the Ghoul."

"He's the what?"

"You heard me. You must hold him here until the marshal arrives."

Harvey stared at James Chatterly, and laughed. "Lady, what do you take me for? A simpleton? It was the Ghoul who everyone thought killed your husband pretty near a year ago, wasn't it? Now you're saying he killed himself?" He laughed some more.

"You don't understand," Helsa said.

"Sure I do," Harvey said. "You're trying to trick me, to confuse me so I won't up and shoot your lover, here." He nodded at Fargo.

"Her what?" James said.

Helsa groaned.

"Her lover," Harvey told James. "I saw them with my own eyes. They were going at it right on your kitchen table."

James looked at her and Helsa looked away. "My, oh my. You're not so innocent, after all."

"My friends saw them too," Harvey said. "But they're dead now, thanks to this son of a bitch." He pointed his rifle at Fargo. "I've come to settle accounts once and for all."

"Then you truly aren't here for me?" James asked.

"Mister, it didn't work with her and it won't work with you. Nothing either of you say or do is going to stop me from making maggot bait of this bastard." Harvey gave Fargo a hard push into the parlor and Fargo stumbled several steps. "I have hardly slept or eaten for dreaming of this."

James grinned at Helsa. "We all have our little secrets, don't we, my sweet?"

"He was the first and only," Helsa said. "It had been so long."

"No need to explain. I hardly have the right to judge you, now do I?"

Harvey was growing mad. "What are you two talking about?" He shook his head. "Forget it. I don't want to know. What I want is for both of you to shut the hell up while I work out what to do with you."

"You're not going to shoot us?" James asked.

"I have nothing against you or her. It's him I'm after." Again Harvey indicated Fargo.

James Chatterly laughed. "Life is too peculiar for words."

"Please, Harvey," Helsa said. "I'm being truthful. My husband *is* the Ghoul. He has killed four women and others. The marshal and most of the men went out after him and will be back any moment. Turn him over to them and the whole town will be grateful."

"You don't know when to shut up," Harvey said.

"You'll be a hero," Helsa persisted. "Please. For all our sakes. Take him to the jail and wait for the marshal."

"You'd like that, wouldn't you? For me to make a fool of myself. Tibbit will arrest me on sight. Then you can brag to everyone how you pulled the wool over my eyes."

"No, no, no," Helsa said.

"Enough," Harvey exploded. "Not another peep out of you. I've never hurt a woman but you're testing my patience."

James said to Fargo, "Isn't this glorious?"

"Enough out of you, too," Harvey said to him. He took a step and centered the muzzle on Fargo's chest. "You can talk, though. You can beg me to spare you. Not that I will but I want to hear it."

"Go to hell," Fargo said.

James Chatterly laughed.

"Please, Mr. Stansfield," Helsa pleaded. "You must believe me. Yes, I admit what you said about Mr. Fargo and me. But I'm not making it up about my husband. With God as my witness, he really is the Ghoul. *I'm begging you.* Please, please, please, turn him over to the marshal."

Harvey Stansfield was slow to respond, and for a few moments Fargo thought she had convinced him. He should have known better.

"You know what? I've changed my mind. It wouldn't be too smart of me to kill Fargo and leave witnesses." Harvey chuckled. "I'm going to kill all three of you." He sighted down the barrel at Fargo and then swung the barrel toward James and then at Helsa in the rocking chair. "The question is, which one of you lunkheads do I shoot first?" He centered the barrel on Fargo again. "Can you guess who it will be?"

20

James Chatterly put his hands on his hips and threw back his head and roared with mirth.

"What the hell is the matter with you?" Harvey Stansfield asked. "I just told you I'm going to blow out your wick and you think it's funny?"

"You have no notion," James said.

"I'm beginning to think you're loco."

"He is," Helsa said. "He's insane and vicious and as evil as any man who ever drew breath. For God's sake please listen to me. Please do as I ask and turn him over to the marshal. Or if you won't do that, shoot him."

"What?" Harvey and James said at the same moment.

Before she could reply they all heard the drum of hooves out in the street. They heard a horse whinny—it sounded like the Ovaro to Fargo—and then voices and footsteps on the front porch and a knock on the door. The door opened, and only Fargo, standing in the parlor entryway, saw who entered: Marshal Tibbit, Sam Worthington, and Tom Wilson. The lawman saw him, and smiled.

"Fargo! There you are. The rest of the posse is bringing in the bodies but we came on ahead. I wanted to talk to you about the Ghoul."

As Tibbit talked he came down the hall with the farmer and the townsman trailing behind. At the sight of Stansfield and the Chatterlys he drew up short in consternation. "What's this?" he demanded, staring at the rifle Harvey was holding. "What's going on here?"

"Thank God," Helsa said.

For an instant the tableau froze. Fargo was poised to spring. The lawman and Worthington and Wilson were rooted in confusion. Helsa looked relieved that they had arrived. James Chatterly was grinning. Then Harvey Stansfield said, "Damn it. I'm not letting you stop me, Marshal. Not this time you won't."

And Harvey jerked his rifle to his shoulder.

Fargo dived to his left and drew as he dived. He fired at the same moment Harvey did; Harvey's slug tore into the floor while Fargo's slug smashed Harvey back against the wall. Helsa screamed. James Chatterly was also in motion, his hand sweeping under his black jacket and reappearing with a pocket pistol. He squeezed off a shot at Tibbit. Blood burst from Tibbit's left shoulder and the lawman staggered back, bleating like a kicked sheep. Worthington and Wilson came to life, each clawing for his revolver. Neither were gun hands. The big farmer barely had his out and the townsman was fumbling with his firearm when James Chatterly banged off two swift shots while backpedaling toward the far side of the room. Fargo fired from the floor at Chatterly and hit him, too. The impact twisted him partway around and he snapped a shot in return that buzzed past Fargo's ear. Without breaking stride, Chatterly threw his arms in front of his face and hurtled at the window. The glass shattered and showered down, and Chatterly was gone.

Tibbit had unlimbered his pistol and was taking aim at Stansfield.

Harvey fired, and the lawman, hit in the belly, doubled over but managed to get off a shot of his own that dug a furrow in the wall. Sam Worthington was on his knees, a big hand over a spreading stain on his shirt. Tom Wilson was prone and not moving except for his twitching legs.

Fargo heaved up. He fired as Harvey Stansfield turned toward him, fired as Stansfield fired, fired as Stansfield crumpled and sank to the floor leaving a crimson smear on the wall. Whirling, Fargo raced across the room and flung himself at the broken window. He cleared the sill and the glass and tucked into a forward roll that brought him up in a crouch on the side of the house.

The Colt was empty. Out of habit he'd had five pills in the wheel and not six. A lot of men didn't load a cartridge under the hammer to prevent their revolvers from accidentally going off if the weapons were jarred. Now he reloaded while flying toward the back of the house. He'd heard a horse. As he came around the corner he saw the back gate open and James Chatterly gripping a saddle horn and about to mount.

Fargo got off a swift shot, and winged him. Chatterly let go of the horn and spun and ran toward a side street, firing as he went.

Fargo flattened but only until the lead stopped searing the air. Then he was up and out the gate. Spooked by the gunfire, the horse was galloping off. James Chatterly was a vague shape in the night, moving remarkably fast for someone who was wounded.

Fargo gave chase. He would be damned if he was letting the man get away again. His boots pounding, he came to the side street. Chatterly had turned up it and was heading for the heart of town. Fargo's feet grew wings.

James Chatterly reached Main Street and glanced back. He slowed, snapped off a shot, then turned and ran—back toward the boardinghouse.

Fargo divined his purpose and poured on the speed. He reached the main street and saw Chatterly climbing onto Marshal Tibbit's mount. Chatterly's teeth were white in the darkness as, reining around, he slapped his legs and galloped to the east.

"No, you don't," Fargo vowed. He sped to the Ovaro and unwrapped the reins from the fence.

Fargo did no such thing. Vaulting into the saddle, he reined eastward and stabbed his spurs. Chatterly was almost out of sight and riding hell-bent for leather. Fargo did the same. The town swept behind them and forest loomed. Fargo fired but knew he had missed. Chatterly looked over his shoulder and flashed his damnable grin. Then the madman was in the trees. Fargo swore and lashed the Ovaro. He was almost to the woods when he realized what he was doing. Hauling on the reins, he slowed to keep from crashing pell-mell into the undergrowth. He went another dozen feet, and stopped. The forest was quiet. Not so much as the hoot of an owl broke the stillness.

James Chatterly had stopped, too.

Fargo sat motionless. Save for the flicking of the Ovaro's ears and tail, the stallion might be a statue. Somewhere in the woodland an animal bleated. A rabbit, Fargo guessed, taken by a meat eater. The wait stretched into a minute, the minute into two. Fargo pricked his ears at a slight rustling, as of a large animal moving slowly. The sound came from north of him. Reining toward it, he rode at a walk. So many black shadows dappled the star-lit vegetation that it was impossible to tell one tree from other or to spot a man if he was cleverly hidden.

Fargo had the Colt cocked and firmly clenched. He raked his gaze up and down and back and forth, alert for the slightest movement. Chatterly had to be there; the rustling had sounded near. He ducked to pass under a low limb and came to a small clearing.

Astride the marshal's mount on the other side sat the Ghoul. He flashed another of his grins. "You are worse than a bloodhound. Most anyone else would not have come after me."

"I'll take that as a compliment." Fargo tingled with expectation of the bloodshed to come.

"How was she?" James asked.

Fargo was so intent on Chatterly's hands that he was slow to catch his meaning. "How was who?"

"You know damn well who. She admitted it. You and her on the kitchen table. How was she?"

"Why bring her up?" Fargo suspected it was to distract him and give Chatterly an edge.

"I can't hardly believe it. Not the kitchen table, I can't."

"She was fine."

Chatterly's grins had become aggravating. "You're just saying that. She never once did it on the table with me. With her it always had to be in bed at night with the lights out."

Fargo had met women like that. He never much cared whether there was light or not. If they wanted to do it in the dark, good and dandy. The important thing was that they wanted to do it.

"Not that she didn't like doing it," James said. "I give her credit for that much."

"Some married men can't even say that," Fargo heard himself say.

"I had it good and didn't realize how good I had it?" James's shoulders rose and fell. "Maybe so. 'The grass always looks greener'—isn't that the saying? But it was more than that. She wouldn't let me whip her. She wouldn't let me tie her up. Hell, she wouldn't let me blindfold her."

"Why the hell are you telling me this?"

"I don't rightly know. Except I don't have long left and I wanted to talk." Chatterly looked down at the front of his shirt. "You hit me back there. Hit me hard. My insides are on fire and I'm bleeding like a stuck pig."

"Good," Fargo said.

"You're almost as mean as me," James Chatterly said. "You probably won't believe this, but I respect that."

"I don't give a damn what you respect."

Chatterly laughed. "Not a shred of sympathy, is there?"

"Not a lick," Fargo said.

"Then I reckon we should get to it. Only . . ." Chatterly paused. "Would you do me a favor?"

"No."

"If you live, would you tell her I'm really and truly sorry? I never hated her. I never meant for her to suffer any."

"You are as pure a son of a bitch as I've ever met."

James sighed. "I reckon I deserve that." He gazed at the stars and then at the benighted forest and finally at Fargo. "One thing though."

Despite himself, Fargo asked, "What?"

"If I am insane"—Chatterly grinned—"I like it." Without warning he jerked his arm up and fired.

Fargo was expecting him to try something and even as the pocket pistol was rising he jabbed his spurs and the Ovaro leaped forward at the same instant as the *crack*. Pain seared his shoulder but he could tell without having to look that he had only been grazed and he was in the trees and circling before the sound of the shot died. He thought that the Ghoul would try to run off but Chatterly had other ideas; he came charging across the clearing, his pistol blazing. Fargo reined away and weaved among the boles like a four-legged needle threading through a tapestry.

Chatterly came after him, firing with grim intent.

The hunter had become the hunted. Fargo fled to spare the Ovaro from possible harm. He reined toward a thicket and at the last moment veered and galloped around it, instead. On the other side he drew rein and wheeled the Ovaro back the way he had come. He swept the Colt up just as James Chatterly came galloping around and fired as Chatterly sought to take aim, fired as Chatterly clutched at his throat, fired as Chatterly swayed.

The Ghoul pitched to the ground.

Fargo was off the stallion and over to the madman before Chatterly could rise. Not that he ever would; dark rivulets seeped from five or six wounds.

Incredibly, Chatterly wasn't dead. His lips moved and he made a supreme effort to speak. "Remember the favor."

"Go to hell."

James Chatterly grinned. "On my way," he said, and died.

A quarter of an hour later Fargo drew rein at the picket fence. The street, to his surprise, was deserted. Yet people had to have heard the shots. He opened the gate and went on in. The smell of fresh blood was strong. "Helsa?" he called out.

No one answered.

A pair of legs jutted from the parlor. It was Wilson, face-down in a halo of scarlet. Past him, vacant eyes fixed on the ceiling, lay Marshal Marion Tibbit.

Sam Worthington was on his side, his big hands over his belly. His eyes were shut and his teeth clenched and he was shaking but not making any sounds. Harvey Stansfield had fallen in a crumpled heap. Over in the rocking chair sat Helsa, slumped in despair.

"Helsa?" Fargo said again. When she didn't respond he stepped over Tibbit and around Stansfield to the rocking chair. A pink hole high on her forehead stopped him cold. "Damn," he said. He stepped to Worthington and hunkered. "Sam?"

The farmer's eyes were pools of torment. "Tell me you got him. Tell me I'm not dying for nothing."

"You're not dying for nothing," Fargo said.

"Good." Worthington coughed up blood, and grimaced. "That damn Stansfield. I hope he's dead, too."

Fargo glanced at the heap and nodded.

"Will you do me a favor?"

"It's my night for them."

"Eh?"

"Whatever you want," Fargo said.

"Go to my farm. Let my wife and my young'uns know that . . ." Worthington sucked in a deep breath.

"Maybe I should go for the doc. Where does he live?"

"I'll be hogswaggled," Worthington said.

"What do you want me to tell your family?" Fargo asked when he didn't go on. But the farmer was past answering. "Hell." Fargo closed the man's eyes and rose and stepped back to survey the slaughter just as the heap sat bolt upright and a rifle was pointed at him.

"I have you now," Harvey Stansfield declared. Red drops were trickling from the corners of his mouth.

"You are persistent," Fargo said.

"You bet your ass I am. I refuse to die until I take you with me."

"There's only one problem."

"What?" Harvey said.

"You're slow as hell, and stupid to boot." Fargo drew and put a slug squarely in the middle of Stansfield's forehead. The rifle went off but the ceiling took the lead. Walking over, Fargo kicked the rifle away and felt for a pulse. As if there was any doubt.

At that time of night Fargo had the trail to the west to himself, and he was glad. He'd had enough of people to last him a good long spell. Squaring his shoulders, he rode from the heart of human darkness into the blackness of the wilds, and it was like coming home.

LOOKING FORWARD!
The following is the opening
section of the next novel in the exciting
Trailsman **series from Signet:**

THE TRAILSMAN #351
TERROR TOWN

The Smoky Mountains, 1861—where strangers
who aren't careful wind up six feet under.

The two men with rifles came out of the trees as Fargo was
filling his first cup of morning coffee. That they came up on
him so quietly wasn't a good sign. That he was still sluggish
from sleep didn't help, either. He should have heard them.
He stayed calm and regarded them as if they were passersby
on a street. "Gents," he said simply.

One was older than the other by a good many years. Judging by their faces and builds they were father and son. Their
clothes were homespun, their boots scuffed, their hats the
kind farmers favored.

The youngest planted himself and thrust his jaw out. "What
are you doing here, mister?"

"Having breakfast," Fargo said. He set down the coffeepot and held the tin cup in his left hand while lowering his

right hand to his side, and his holster. It was on the side away from them and they didn't notice.

"You're not from Promise?"

"Is that a settlement?" Fargo asked. So many new ones were springing up he didn't bother to keep track.

"Did the marshal send you?"

"Boy, I just told you I don't know the place," Fargo said.

His right hand brushed his Colt.

"How do we know you're not lying? How do we know you're not here to arrest us?"

"Do you see a star on my shirt, lunkhead?" Fargo snapped. He was in no mood for this. Some mornings he tended to be grumpy until he had his coffee.

The young one colored red in the cheeks. "You shouldn't ought to talk to me like that."

"Then you should grow a brain."

That did it. The young one turned entirely red and started to jerk his rifle.

Fargo had the Colt out and cocked before the rifle moved an inch. "How dumb are you?"

The young one froze, his eyes widening in fear.

"Simmer down, Samuel," the older man said. "He ain't no lawman. If he was here to harm us, you'd be dead." The older man smiled. "I'm Wilt Flanders."

"Means nothing to me." Fargo wagged the Colt. "Have your son set down his rifle. Nice and slow."

"I will not," Samuel said. "And, Pa, how's he know you and me are related if he's not from Promise?"

"Use your head, son," Wilt said. "Do like the man wants and maybe we'll live through this."

Sulkily, Samuel bent and placed his rifle on the ground and straightened. "I don't like this."

"Then you shouldn't go around pointing guns at people." Fargo trained the Colt on the father. "Now you, old man."

"Be glad to." Wilt did as his son had and held his arms out from his sides. "There. No need for lead chucking. Suppose we just talk."

Fargo took a sip of coffee and savored the heat that spread down his gullet and into the pit of his stomach. "For nearly spoiling my breakfast I should shoot you anyway."

"Pa!" Samuel said, and glanced down at his rifle.

"He's joshing, son. Stand still and be quiet while I talk to him."

"He treats me like I'm stupid," Samuel pouted.

"Hush now, son." Wilt gestured at Fargo. "Can I come close and sit?"

"No."

"Fair enough." Wilt cleared his throat. "We have a small farm down this hill and out on the prairie a piece. We're up here after deer."

"Why would you think I was a marshal?"

"We've had some trouble with the law in Promise," Wilt said. "It's to the north, about half a day's ride."

"What sort of trouble?" Not that Fargo cared. He just wanted them to be gone so he could finish his breakfast in peace.

"My Martha refuses to wear a bonnet when she goes into town."

Fargo wasn't sure he'd heard correctly. "Martha being your wife, I take it?"

"Yes, sir."

"What the hell does a bonnet have to do with anything?"

"It's against town ordinance for a female to be out in public without one on her head."

Fargo would have thought the farmer was joking if not for his earnest expression. "That is about the damned silliest thing I've ever heard."

Wilt smiled. "My Martha feels the same way. She says a woman should have the right to cover her head or not."

"Why would they pass such a law?"

"You go into Promise, you'll understand quick enough," Wilt said. "But I wouldn't advise it. They don't cotton to strangers much."

"Is that a fact?"

"My pa never lies, mister," Samuel bristled.

"I wasn't saying he did, peckerwood." Fargo sipped more coffee.

"The last time we were in town," Wilt went on, "the marshal told us we have to pay a dollar fine for Martha not wearing her bonnet. We had five days to pay. It's been seven and we haven't so it's likely they'll send someone to collect."

"Over our dead bodies," Samuel said.

"I won't tell you again to be quiet," Wilt said.

Fargo twirled the Colt into his holster. "You can pick up your rifles and go on with your hunt. I reckon I'll fight shy of this Promise. There are enough nuisances in my life." He gave Samuel a pointed glance.

"You'll have to swing pretty wide," Wilt said. "There's the town and the farms and a few ranches around it. Could take you a day or two out of your way."

Fargo didn't like the idea of the delay. He watched closely as the pair reclaimed their long guns. Both had the presence of mind to keep the barrels pointed down. "Off you go," he said.

They turned and went to the trees and Wilt paused to look back. "If you change your mind, be careful, you hear? I wasn't kidding about them not liking strangers. Any excuse they can come up with to give you a hard time, they will."

Father and son hiked off. Fargo kept his right hand close to his Colt until they were out of sight. He sat back, opened his saddlebags, and took out a bundle wrapped in rabbit fur.

Opening it, he helped himself to several pieces of pemmican.

He liked pemmican more than jerky. The berries mixed with the ground meat and the fat lent it a zesty taste.

The sun was half an hour high when Fargo got under way. He held the Ovaro to a walk until he was out of the hills and then brought it to a trot until he came to a rutted road and a sign.

He drew rein and read it out loud.

"Promise. Twenty miles. The cleanest little town west of the Mississippi." Fargo scratched his beard. Frontier towns were notorious for the windblown dust that got into everything, and for droppings in their streets. To have one boast of being clean was a novelty.

Fargo rode on. Now and then he passed farmhouses and a few cabins. In ten miles he came on a fork and another sign. It said the same thing and added in smaller letters, "Stable service. Saloon open noon until midnight. Preachers welcome. Drummers and patent medicine men are not."

"Well now," Fargo said. He had a decision to make; go around or ride on through. Since he didn't much like the idea of losing a day or two, he went on. The mention of a saloon helped persuade him. It had been a week since his last drink and he would dearly love some whiskey.

A mile out Fargo came on yet another sign, the biggest and grandest yet. It mentioned that Promise had a population of one hundred and twelve souls. Harry Bascomb was mayor. Lloyd Travers was marshal.

"Good to know," Fargo said, and grinned. He'd seldom come across a town so full of itself. Gigging the stallion, he continued to the outskirts. He'd expected a quiet little hamlet with a few horses at hitch rails and not a lot of people moving about. Instead, to his consternation, the street was lined with parked farm wagons and buckboards and there had to be thirty horses tied off. Folks were everywhere, strolling about, peering in store windows and whatnot. A lot were families with kids.

A celebration of some sort, Fargo reckoned, and gigged the Ovaro. He was conscious of the stares thrown his way. But he was a stranger and that was normal.

The sole saloon was next to the general store. It was called Abe's, and the rail out front was full. Fargo reined around to the side and dismounted. He arched his back to relieve a kink and let the reins dangle. The Ovaro wouldn't go anywhere.

A stream of people flowed along the boardwalk. Fargo touched his hat to a pair of young ladies in bright dresses and bonnets who grinned and giggled and sashayed on by. He looked around and saw that all the females wore bonnets, even the smallest girls.

Fargo pushed on the batwings. The familiar scents of liquor and cigar smoke and the clink of poker chips made him glad he had stopped. The place was packed. He shouldered to the bar and smacked the counter and a bartender with a bushy mustache and a big smile came over.

"What will it be, stranger?"

"Whiskey." Fargo fished a coin from his pocket. As the bartender produced a glass and poured, he motioned and said, "It's not the Fourth of July, is it?" He didn't make it a habit to keep up with the calendar.

The bartender chuckled. "Sure isn't. All this to-do is because of the hanging."

"The what?" Fargo said, although he'd heard perfectly well.

"Everyone is in town to see Steve Lucas strung up." The bartender glanced at a clock above the shelves behind the bar.

"In about an hour. I'll be closing so I can go. It's not every day you get to see someone swing."

"No, it's not," Fargo said. The times he had, he tried to forget. It was an awful way to die.

"The mayor is going to give a speech and there are booths where you can buy juice and cakes and pie."

"Nothing like a hanging to work up an appetite," Fargo said.

About to turn away, the bartender gave him a sharp look.

"I don't know as I like your tone. The man being hung deserves it. He was caught red-handed."

"Caught doing what?"

It wasn't the bartender who answered. It was a tall, lanky man in a broad-brimmed black hat and a vest with a star on it.

"Rustling."

Fargo turned. "Marshal Travers, I take it?"

The lawman nodded. He had a long, bony face and close-set eyes. "I found the cow myself in his barn."

"*One* cow?"

"One or twenty, it's all the same. Lucas stole it and he has to pay." Travers leaned on an elbow. "You here for the necktie social or some other reason?"

Fargo treated himself to a swallow of Monongahela. "For this. Then I aim to be on my way."

"Make sure you stay out of trouble. You won't like what happens if you don't."

Fargo held his temper in check and said, "You're not very friendly."

"We have a nice town here and we like to keep it that way,"

Marshal Travers said, and smiled. "So no, we're not very friendly at all."

No other series packs this much heat!

THE TRAILSMAN